# SPACEHAWKS

## BOOK 2: ASSASSINS

ED SUTTER

WHISKEY CREEK PRESS
www.whiskeycreekpress.com

Stephen,
you can close your eyes
during the scary parts!
Ed

Published by
WHISKEY CREEK PRESS
Whiskey Creek Press
PO Box 51052
Casper, WY 82605-1052
www.whiskeycreekpress.com



eISBN: 978-1-61160-874-8
Print ISBN: 978-1-63355-739-0

**Cover Artist: Susan Krupp**
**Editor: Jeremy Tyler**
**Printed in the United States of America**

# Chapter 1: Belle of the Ball

Jason Hawke ran his finger around the inside of the collar of his dress blues. There must be some way to make this damned uniform more comfortable! The Marine Corps tended to make their uniforms exceedingly snug, perhaps to show off the fitness of their wearers, but that close-fitting style certainly didn't make them easier to wear. Most of his Marine Corps service had involved wearing field uniforms, which were rugged, durable, and way more comfortable for the wearers. They weren't very pretty though.

His new wife, Kristin Baird, watched him and giggled. "It won't strangle you. I promise. I made that one of the most important criteria when I talked to the tailors. 'Make sure it doesn't cut off the flow of air to his brain. He needs all the brain cells he's got left!' I told them."

"Thanks a bunch," he said sarcastically. Then he smiled. He couldn't help but smile when he looked at his wife, but then he put on a mock-stern expression. "Of course, you're in no danger of strangling yourself in that dress. Falling out of it, maybe, but not strangling."

The Confederation Senator looked down at herself. Her navy blue spaghetti-strapped gown flowed in a sea of silk and lace, with, of course, a deeply cut bodice. Strappy high-heeled sandals peeped out from beneath the hem. She looked back up at him. "I'll have you know that I am dressed in the height of retro fashion, sir! Besides, you look positively scrumptious in your uniform."

She openly admired his six foot two frame and his broad shoulders. The uniform made his muscularity very obvious.

It was his turn to look down at his own outfit. He'd been out of the Confederation Marine Corps for several years now, but at the special request of the Moderator of the Confederation and, even more importantly, the Commandant of the Marine Corps, he'd had a new set of officer's dress blues made. Somewhat to his disgust, they had also requested, somewhat pointedly, that he wear his medals. All his medals. Now, the left side of his uniform blouse looked like it might stop a bullet, there was so much shiny metal hanging there.

"You look gorgeous," said Kristin. She stepped close and kissed him.

He looked down at Kristin, all five feet and one hundred pounds of her, and smiled.

"Correction. You look gorgeous. I look like a dressed up, trained monkey." He paused. "And not all that well trained, at that."

She laughed with him.

He looked around him. "Well, at least this whole political shebang is almost over."

Kristin nodded. "True, but don't forget. We're invited to after-dinner cocktails with the Moderator and his wife."

"You know I don't drink." He'd gone on a multiple-year binge after he'd gotten out of the Corps, before he'd re-met Kristin and saved her from pirates, and he had no desire to go back to that booze-soaked former life. So these days, he just didn't drink at all.

"Oh poop!" his wife said, "You can just sit around looking beautiful, and let me do the talking."

"That would be me. Sitting around and looking beautiful!"

About fifteen minutes later, the couple was escorted by a member of the Moderator's Bodyguard to a cozy lounge. Moderator of the Confederation of Planets, James Brown, and his wife, Astrid, met them at the door.

Brown shook hands with Kristin first.

"Senator Baird, it's so nice of you to come." He looked over at his wife, who took her turn at shaking Kristin's hand, along with a quick hug. The Moderator said, in an amused voice, "I'm still getting used to calling Kristin by her family name of Baird. I'd just barely gotten to the point of calling her Dunvegan."

He then turned and shook Jason's hand as well. "Captain, are you planning on changing our girl's name again?"

Hawke smiled inwardly at how he knew Kristin would react to being referred to as "our girl." It put a smile on his face as he replied, "No time soon, Sir. Kristin decided to stick with her family name this time."

Kristin chimed in, "and Jason decided to stick with his maiden name as well."

They all laughed. The Moderator gestured at a grouping of comfortable chairs on the far side of the room, and they went over there and had a seat. A steward appeared and asked, "drinks for anyone?"

Brown and his wife each ordered wine, as did Kristin. Never having met a wine he could stand, Hawke declined in favor of water. Besides, the evening was getting late, and in this rarefied atmosphere, he didn't want to put a foot wrong verbally, even assuming that he still imbibed.

When the drinks had been delivered, Brown told the steward, "that'll be all, Richard. We can fend for ourselves from here on out."

The man nodded. "Thank you, Sir. And good night to you all."

Once the door had closed behind Richard, Brown said, "I hate to bring up business so late at night, Kristin, but I needed to talk to you about these latest Navy appropriations."

Kristin was a very junior Senator, but she had very strong family connections that had resulted in gaining her a place on the prestigious Military Services Committee. Like many republican governments, the real work, not to mention the real power, resided in special committees, and the Military Services Committee was arguably the most powerful of all.

However, as a junior Senator, Kristin had a fairly low profile, and Jason figured that was the point of this invitation. If the Moderator had asked to see the Chairman of the Committee in private, tongues would have been wagging. This was a backdoor way of getting a feel for what the Military Services Chairman was thinking, and to perhaps send a message back to him, semi-invisibly.

Then, they heard shots in the corridor.

"Oh shit. Here we go again!" Jason muttered.

With a few moves, he tore off his tight-fitting uniform jacket and pulled off the khaki tie beneath it. He was unbuttoning the collar of the khaki dress shirt when the door slammed open and one of the Bodyguard detail came flying through it backwards, his face a bloody mess. He hit the floor, either unconscious or dead. It looked like he'd not even had a chance to draw his weapon.

A man dressed in a deep forest-green, stretchy-looking outfit came in behind him, moving arrogantly but with smooth power. His hands were bloody.

Jason said dryly, "Not the butler, I presume?"

He didn't wait for an answer, but moved forward to meet the killer.

The man in green was blindingly fast as he closed with Hawke. With a sneer, he launched a fist at the ex-Marine's head, but Jason sidestepped smoothly and punched the guy in the ribs. The blow made his hand hurt and didn't seem to faze Mister Green at all. The killer swung a powerful back-fist that Jason took on his shoulder. The blow knocked him backwards and off his feet. Green came after him quickly to finish him off. But Jason rolled away from the incoming front snap kick and came to his knees. When the killer launched himself at the kneeling Hawke, Jason came up from the floor, all the strength of his legs and arm thrusting up into one punch. He bellowed a kiai shout as he rose.

Jason's right fist met Mister Green's jaw right at its point, and it really hurt his fist. What was this guy made of, metal?

But the massive blow snapped the killer's head back sharply, and there was a sodden snap as his neck broke. Mister Green dropped to the floor, dead.

Jason was cradling his right hand in his left, wondering if he'd broken it when a noise from the door caused him to pivot in that direction.

Another green-clad killer rushed into the room. He took one look at his comrade's body on the floor and another at Jason Hawke. With a scream, he charged, coming like a high-speed aircar out of control.

Instantly forgetting how much his hand hurt, Jason spun out of the way of Green Two. This time, he resolved to not use his fists. These guys must be wearing body armor or something, but they could be killed.

As the killer swept by him, the momentum of his killing punch taking him off his balance, Jason raked the man's eyes with his fingernails.

The Green Boy's eyes weren't armored, and he bellowed in shock and pain. Nevertheless, the new killer responded with a powerful backfist that, again, Jason slid by. He hand darted in and out in a lightning quick strike, and the killer lost one eye completely. This time Green Two screamed. Before he could recover, Jason was behind him, and grabbing the man by the back of his shaven head and his chin, with a powerful twist, he broke this killer's neck as well. Hawke let the body drop lifeless to the carpet.

Looking up, Jason saw that Kristin had armed herself with the dead Bodyguard's pulser pistol and was pointing it at the door, her hands rock steady.

They waited, but there were no more screams of gunshots. In a few minutes that seemed a whole lot longer, a contingent of Moderatorial Bodyguards showed up, guns drawn.

Kristin put the pistol down and came to Jason's arms.

He said, "and here I thought all this political stuff was boring!"

Still holding his wife, Jason looked over at the leader of the Bodyguard detail, he asked, "Who were these guys, anyway?"

The man had been watching the examination of the two Green's bodies, but now he looked over at Hawke.

"I don't know yet, sir, but we will find out." He paused. "And good work here, Sir."

"Thanks, I think."

# Chapter 2: Conspiracy

*Three Months Before: Desotoan Empire*

The agent looked closely at the man he knew as the Director of Foreign Operations for the Desotoan Empire's Security Services and asked, "am I to assume that the Emperor has approved these activities?"

The Director, Don Enrique Mendoza, gave the man a cold look. "The Emperor has stated his goals in this matter. He has no wish to know the mundane details of how we achieve those goals."

The agent nodded in understanding. Plausible deniability was a long-standing pillar of covert operations for star nations. Aloud, he said, "as the Emperor wishes, so shall it be done."

Mendoza asked, “So by what agency do you plan to execute those goals?”

The agent, really a spymaster by the name of Edouardo Lopez, answered with careful generalities. “I am making contact with two organizations to ‘execute’, as you so carefully put it, this mission. One contact is the one known as the Old Man on Alamut. The other is the House Hawke, on Old Terra. Both have excellent reputations.”

Mendoza nodded. He had heard of these people over the years. They were indeed effective at what they did. And what they did was assassination. “And if they refuse?”

“They may then become a possible leak. They will be eliminated.”

“That may not be so easy.”

It was Lopez’s turn to nod. “True, but anyone can be taken, if sufficient force is applied.”

“True. Very well. Carry on. Your mission is a go.”

“And the other parts of the plan?” asked Lopez.

“That is none of your concern.”

People, enemies of the Desotoan Empire, were going to die.

And it was good.

# Chapter 3: House Hawke

*One Month Before: Old Terra*

The terrain behind the sprawling house was mountainous. Nestled in the shadow of the Rocky Mountains on the continent of NorAm on Old Terra, the family center of the House Hawke looked like other ranch houses in the region, but its income did not come from cattle or grain. It came from killing.

The House Hawke was centuries old, and it trained its sons in the art of assassination. They were the best of the best. Hawkes didn't hire out for your local mob hits; they were generally employed only by governments, and their rates were very high. Of course, the fact that they never failed helped.

The current generation had taken a different course, however, or different courses. Of the four sons, only one had remained in the traditional family business. That one son, Cuchulain Hawke, heard the tone that let him know they were about to have visitors.

His communicator beeped about a microsecond later. "Koo?"

"On it, Dad," he replied.

Koo moved to a firing position near the far right corner of the front wall of the house. That way, he could enfilade an attack heading toward the front door. He knew that his father, Temujin Hawke, would be posted near the main entrance, and that his mother would take up post near the rear.

He heard his Dad's voice again. "Koo, are you expecting anybody today?"

"Negative. You?"

"Nope. But let's not assume they're hostiles until they show their hand. This could be just somebody's messenger boy."

"Or girl," Tomiko Hawke chimed in.

"Granted," said Temujin in a dry tone. "On the other hand, it could be someone who we've offended in the past or even a counter-assassination squad."

Koo was puzzled. "But we don't have a contract right now, that I know of."

His father replied, "True, but it could be preemptive. Anyway, we'll find out soon enough."

Koo called up his heads-up display, one of many sensor options in the headset he was wearing. The HUD gave him a real-time image of the road leading to the house. He saw a large, expensive-looking Mercedes ground effect car coming in their direction. As he'd been trained, however, as soon as he spotted the potential threat in front of him, he began scanning everywhere else, including above.

"Dad, I've got two large aircars hovering just out of visual range. I also think I'm getting a reading on a drone at about ten thousand feet above our position."

"I've got 'em. Good job, Koo." Temujin had, in fact already spotted the additional vehicles; whether they were threats, targets, or just a security detail. Of course, they could be all three.

"Okay," said the patriarch of the Hawke clan, "I'm going to go out and talk to this incoming gentleman. Stay alert."

Cuchulain kept a sniper rifle up to the firing port, while also keeping one eye on his HUD. The (presumably) manned aircraft were loitering at extreme range, and the drone was in orbit above the ranch.

As the gleaming black Mercedes came into the circular drive before the front doors, Temujin stepped out onto the covered porch. There were no weapons in his hands, although with a member of the Hawke family, that didn't mean much.

The rear doors opened and a slim man in an expensive suit got out of one side. From the other door, a beefy bodyguard type emerged. It was clear to Hawke that the latter man was carrying weapons of some sort.

The slim man came up the steps to the porch wearing a smile that Temujin associated with used aircar salesmen. The man extended his hand, saying, "Mister Hawke, I presume?"

Hawke nodded, but did not offer his hand. After a moment, the newcomer's smile wilted a bit, and he lowered his hand.

"So what might you have come way out here for?" asked Hawke.

The man nodded. "Mister Hawke, I have a business offer for House Hawke."

Temujin's expression never changed. Although there had never been much doubt, the mention of House Hawke pretty much defined what the business might entail. "And that business offer might be?"

The man blinked, clearly a bit nonplused, but he forged ahead. "Mister Hawke, a certain party would like to employ House Hawke to dispose of a problem for them."

"By 'dispose,' I assume you mean kill. Who is this employer?"

The gofer shook his head. "They wish to remain anonymous."

Hawke's face remained stony. "Then we do not have a deal. I do not work for unknown employers."

"But, Mister Hawke…"

"Good-bye," Temujin said. He turned to walk into the house.

He detected movement behind him, pivoted, and threw a knife twenty yards, taking the burly bodyguard in the left eye. The man screamed and dropped the pulser pistol he had begun to raise.

Hawke looked at the man in the suit. "Are you still here?"

The man looked over at the dead body, and then back at Hawke. He turned ghost white and hustled over to the car. He climbed in, and the aircar was moving before he had fully closed the door.

Entering the house, Temujin got on the house-band and said, "unless I miss my guess, we are going to have company very shortly."

He continued, "Koo, cover the air threats. Tomiko, you and I will watch the perimeter."

Koo was already on his HUD, and almost immediately, he saw the two aircraft starting to close on the house at speed.

"Airborne threats closing," he reported, "Engaging."

With a command to his wrist comm, Koo engaged the air defense systems that had been built into the house years ago. Like a sovereign nation, House Hawke had a special dispensation from the Confederation and local Terran authorities to arm themselves. It gave a whole new meaning to the term, "home defense."

Three missile batteries arose from mounds around the house, and in a flash, literally, Mach 8 projectiles were flying toward the aircraft that Koo had locked into their machine brains. Three explosions flared in the sky over that little part of Colorado.

There was gunfire from the rear of the house, so Koo rushed in that direction, although he left his HUD active, just in case of more threats. The Hawke family trained in a very hard school.

Koo called out, "Mom, Koo coming up behind you!"

As he rounded the last corner, Tomiko Hawke was taking a high-velocity smokepole-type rifle with a high-tech scope from her shoulder. She turned to him and said, "Oh, hi, Cuchulain. No problem here."

He looked out of the nearby window and saw at least five bodies in the open space between the house and the forest. He laughed. "Not anymore, anyway. Good shooting."

She gave him a bland look and said, "What did you expect? I'm a Hawke, too."

Temujin came on the house band and said, "Koo, get on the computer and track that idiot. I put a tracer in the back end of his car while he was gawking at his dead bodyguard. Let's see where he goes."

He gave a hard laugh. "We may want to pay him a visit."

# Chapter 4: On the Border

Kat Dunvegan was happy and in her element. She was flying a hot space fighter right to the edge of its envelope in combat with other hot pilots.

Of course, this was only a mock dogfight, and no one was really trying to kill her, and that was overall a good thing. A small part of her missed the clarity and intensity of real combat. For that matter, she wasn't even in the Confederation Space Navy any more. She was out here on the border as a consultant, advising on fighter tactics against top-of-the-line Desotoan fighter spacecraft.

Two years before, she had borrowed—well, stolen—a Desotoan El Cid fighter. When the other, legitimate, Desotoan pilots had gotten airborne, they had registered their indignation by trying to shoot her down, with extreme prejudice. Kat had responded by not only shooting down the fighters that had attacked her, but by also destroying the rest of the squadron on the ground. Quite a bit of the base had been vaporized in the process as well. Oh well, she figured, you can't please everyone!

Once the Confed Navy had debriefed her and discovered that she had current stick time not only in flying a front-line Desotoan fighter, but also in dogfighting with the self-same bad guys, they had proposed the whole "consultant" thing. Kat had been wooed by the exceptionally lucrative contract they had waved in front of her, and here she was mock-dogfighting with some Navy and Marine hotshots. She had found that it really embarrassed the Regular Navy types when she waxed their tails.

In this current exercise, she'd blasted toward one of Achaea's moons, but once she'd gotten to the other side, she'd cut engines and gone totally Emcon silent. Using the moon's gravity to slingshot her craft around, back toward the planet, she did a passive scan to find the fighter who'd been tailing her.

Ah, there he was. As the aggressor crossed her bow, Spacecat lit up her active sensor suite, painting the other craft and locking all her weapons systems onto him. In her helmet, she heard her opponent say, "Oh, shit!"

He'd gone on to add a lot of other terms that his mother probably wouldn't approve of.

The referee came on the band and said, “Renfrew, you are toast. Good job, Spacecat.”

Time for a cold one at the Officers’ Club. She headed planetward. Lieutenant Renfrew would be buying.

A voice from behind her shoulder said, “You’ve really been kicking those shavetails’ butts out there, Miz Dunvegan.”

She turned. The speaker was a tall, muscular Confederation Marine light colonel. He was quite handsome, and she got the distinct impression that he was used to women falling into his arms, or whatever. Kat wasn’t particularly interested, but she resolved to remain polite. After all, the Navy, and therefore the Marine Corps, was her employer.

But that didn’t mean that she had to be less than truthful.

“It’s true, Colonel.” A Marine lieutenant colonel was equivalent to a Navy commander. From long tradition, the ranks in the Confed military were derived from the ancient Noram armed services, no matter how illogical that might be in the modern day. The armed forces tended to be conservative and somewhat, some would say, overly tradition-bound. “I’m afraid the local boys have been playing with each other for too long. It’ll do them some good to go up against other tactics and other ways of thinking. After all, you can’t always depend on an enemy doing what you expect them to do.”

He nodded, smiling.

"And that's just why we call them 'the enemy,'" he finished the old line. He stuck out his hand and said, "I'm Lieutenant Colonel Gareth Blaustein. Please call me Gary." He paused. "So, in your encounter with the Desotoan pilots on Bishti, how did you find their competency?"

"Oh, they were good, all right. In fact, one of them darn near nailed me."

His expression clearly said that he'd like to nail her himself, but all he said was, "And I assume that you nailed him instead?"

She gave a wicked smile.

"My Dad always told me, 'If you ain't cheatin', you ain't tryin',' so I cheated." They both laughed. "Most of them, I took out on the ground. With that last guy, I think I made him so mad, he got too close. I slammed on the retros and blasted him as he went by."

He nodded. "An old trick."

"But one that still works." She set her empty beer glass down. "And on that note, I need to get going. I'm meeting my boyfriend."

He gave her an odd look. "The guy in the robe is really your boyfriend?"

She lifted one elegant eyebrow. "Yes, he is."

"It's just that, well, he doesn't seem like he'd be your type."

She gave him a dazzling smile. "Oh, Richard has many hidden talents!"

* * * *

"Sensei," said the young man, "I can't figure out that new technique you showed us yesterday."

Richard Hawke nodded. "And which technique are you referring to, Joseph?"

"The one you called a hip drag, Sensei."

Richard explained as he pantomimed the moves. "A classic hip throw is a Judo or Jujitsu move. In it, you grab your opponent by the upper body, either by the shirt, tunic, or across his shoulders. You then pivot, bending at the waist, and pull him over your upper hip, face down. You turn his body before he hits the floor, so he lands face up.

"With a hip drag, which is actually a kung fu move, you trap your opponent's fist and pull him over your upper leg. He can land face down or face up." He turned to face Jose. "So, does that answer your question? Both techniques are designed to use the opponent's strength and force against him, and to put him on the floor, quite hard sometimes."

The young man bowed. "Thank you, Sensei. I think I get it now."

"Good. Go throw people around."

A moment later, the front door of the erstwhile dojo opened, and Kat Dunvegan entered. Richard could see the students surreptitiously eyeing her. Of course, most of the kids were teenage boys, and Kat was quietly gorgeous. She even got some glances from the girls. The female students were probably either checking out the competition, thinking of her as a sexual partner, or simply interested in the teacher's girlfriend.

Admiring her himself, Richard was again impressed with Kat's beauty and vitality. Added to that was her outfit. Given the climate of this part of Achaea, she was wearing fairly short cargo shorts, a midriff-baring tank top, and short hiking boots. But even beyond her looks, she had a considerable aura of personal magnetism that he'd observed, and others picked up on it even if they didn't realize it.

He turned to the students and bowed.

"OK, guys and girls. Class is over for today." He jerked his head in Kat's direction. "My ride's here."

As he neared Kat, she said, "Your ride?"

He kissed her and replied, "In more ways than one."

She broke the clinch, smacked him in the chest with an open palm, and laughed. "And don't you forget it, you big lug!"

As they walked toward her rental aircar, a police ground-effect cruiser stopped nearby and a plainclothes man got out. He saw Kat and Richard and moved purposefully in their direction.

Richard sized him up. The man had a pretty hefty build, along with a cheap suit and a spreading middle, but his eyes were keen and intelligent. He said, "Might you be Richard Hawke?"

Richard gave that man a small bow and nodded. "That I am."

The man said, "Some local muggers have been turning up in the hospitals."

He gave the man a quizzical look.

"Really? That's interesting." He was silent for a moment, and then added, "Overall, I wouldn't think that would be a bad thing."

"Yes. I'm Detective Connelly, and I got saddled with looking into the assaults, if that's what they could really be called," he continued, "And I gather that they were reluctant to admit it, but it seems they had the snot beat out of them by some guy in a robe."

Richard gave the detective a flat look. "Lots of people wear robes."

Connelly nodded. "True, but we've ruled out most of the local priests. Anyway, all I wanted to say was that, if I knew who this guy was, I'd probably congratulate him on a job well done." He nodded to both of them, and said, "Sir, Madam," and then he just walked back to his car.

Barely containing a smile, Kat looked at Richard and said, "Richard, what have you been up to?"

He opened the door to her aircar on his side and replied, "Nothing. Just wandering around the neighborhood and meeting all the friendly people."

"Uh-huh." She got in and they took off. "And were any of those 'friendly people' muggers by any chance?"

He looked pious. "Not any more. I read to them from the Book."

She chuckled. "I'll just bet you did."

# Chapter 5: Assignment

Starcastle was not only the capital planet of the Confederation of Planets; it was also the most sophisticated and exciting city in the galaxy, and Roland Hawke loved it. His rural upbringing on Terra, Old Earth, was a distant memory. His father had more or less disowned him when he took the skills of House Hawke and used them to make a career for himself in business. Granted, the business was security, here read espionage and assassination, but it wasn't Hawke family business, and that made it unforgivable. His father had also written off Jason, Roland's older brother, when he'd joined the Confederation Marine Corps. Taking his banishment as a given, Roland had never even gone back to visit. He felt a bit guilty about that upon occasion, but it was also very freeing. He could be whatever he chose to be, and was not confined by the strictures of the Hawke family.

Galactica Security was the largest security firm in the Confederation, and they frequently received outsourcing missions from the Confed Government, their intelligence services in particular. In theory, despite the exorbitant rates that Galactica charged, the intelligence agencies kept their budgets down and could always point out that they had nothing to do with the most recent incident of espionage or murder. It was a win-win situation.

At the moment, Roland was standing at the large, floor-to-ceiling window of his apartment on the two-hundredth floor of the Starcastle Arms, one of the plushest and most expensive skyscrapers on the planet. He was holding a cup of black tea and was completely naked.

A voice from behind him said, "That must be quite a sight for your neighbors."

Roland turned around. His manager at Galactica Security, Gillian Straley, was equally nude, although she was partially covered by a spider-silk sheet.

He smiled at the sight. Gillian was quite beautiful, and they had been lovers for a couple of years now. They had to keep things very sub rosa, since he did work for her, but the passion was too strong to totally deny.

He replied. "For one thing, the nearest apartment, my 'neighbors' if you will, are a half-mile away and fifty floors down. They'd have to really work at it to see me."

She gave a throaty laugh. "But it would definitely be worth it!" She gave his lean, muscular body an admiring glance, but then sat up and started grabbing clothes. “I’ve got to go. Duty calls.”

“You’re working today?”

She sighed. “Only for a little while. Maybe we can get together tomorrow.”

“Sounds good to me.”

“And quit staring. It’s distracting.”

“Your wish is my command.”

* * * *

Two hours later, as he was finishing his daily workout, Roland’s comm buzzed. It had that annoying shriek of a high priority call, which was never good. Wiping the sweat from his face with a towel, he activated his implant, and a holo of Gillian appeared before him.

“Roland,” she said in a tense voice, “get into the office right now. We have a high-level tasking.”

He threw his towel into the corner. “What’s up?”

“Somebody just tried to kill the Moderator.”

“On my way.”

* * * *

Fifteen minutes later, he entered the door to Gillian’s office. The moment she saw him, she stood, grabbed a data cube or two, and headed for the door. “Let’s go,” she said, “a CI rep is in the conference room down the hall. He’s got all the data, and he also brought a witness to the assassination attempt.”

Roland matched his pace to hers. “A witness? Some Bodyguard dude?”

She glanced over at him without slackening her pace. “I have no idea. He must have a pretty good clearance though, given the level of this tasking.”

“Point taken.”

As they got to the conference room, the door hissed open automatically, sensing their clearance level. No one with less than a Top Secret, Special Circumstances clearance would now be able to enter the room without their permission.

Two men were seated at the central conference table, a holo screen between them. They had apparently been discussing star maps. Both stood and bowed to the Galactica representatives. The man on Roland’s left was lean to the point of emaciation, with haunted eyes. Roland knew him as Thomas McGuire, a very high level mission control agent. The other man with the CI dude was bigger and broader across the shoulders. This one wore a Marine uniform with lots of fruit salad on his chest.

The Marine smiled and said, “Hello, Roland. It’s good to see you.”

It was his brother, Jason.

Things clicked behind Roland’s eyes. “So you’re the witness?”

His brother nodded. “I am. I was there.”

As though no one in the room knew who he was, the other man said, “I’m Thomas Mcguire, from Central Intelligence. You brother is too modest. He personally killed two of the assassins and saved the Moderator’s life.”

Gillian looked at Jason appraisingly. Roland hadn't told her a lot about his family, and the brothers didn't look much alike, but it appeared to her that they had some things in common.

Roland gave a small smile. "Teach them to go up against a Hawke. Who sent them?"

McGuire said, "We're not sure yet."

But Jason interrupted him before he could say any more. "They were Hashishiyun."

Roland's eyes got bigger. "The Old Man? Alamut? The Assassins?"

Jason nodded with a wry smile. "The very same."

Temujin Hawke had made sure that the boys knew all about any other organized groups of assassins in the Confederation as well as other star systems. They were, if nothing else, competitors, and in some cases, opponents. This would seem to be one of those latter cases.

Roland said, "Well, shit."

Gillian said, "Assassins?"

Roland turned to her and said, "Although they are known by different names, they are most widely known as the Hashishiyun. The Assassins are an ages-old organization that we rather thought had become extinct. Some years ago, however, they once again reared their ugly head. They're based on the planet of Alamut, in the Elburz Sector."

McGuire asked, "Elburz? So they aren't Desotoan?"

Roland shook his head. "Maybe. Maybe not. They started as a sort of self-defense force, I guess. They were surrounded by more powerful neighbors." He paused. "Look, let's have a seat. This is going to take a little while."

When everyone had been seated, he nodded at Jason. "Bro, you were always more interested in this sort of thing than I was. Why don't you take it from here?"

Jason nodded and said, "Okay. Like Roland said, the Assassins started out as a sort of self-defense for a poor planet surrounded by enemies. But their leader, Hassan-i-Sabbah, chose a novel way of defending their territory. Instead of investing in a huge army, which his world couldn't afford, he trained a corps of killers, assassins, to take on their enemies." He looked around at the others. "They were successful. The surrounding governments decided to leave them alone, once several anti-Alamut politicians met with untimely ends. It was decided that it was easier to ignore the Assassins, even to pay them off, than to worry about silent daggers in the night."

McGuire said, "But as far as I know, the Confederation is no threat to anybody on Alamut. We're not even interested in the Elburz Sector. It's poor, and it isn't strategically placed."

Jason smiled and replied, "Ah, but that's the rub. The Assassins were so successful, that they began to hire out their operatives, their Fida'I, to other governments. Basically, they went into the business of murder."

Gillian said, "Nasty."

Jason said, "Oh, it gets better. About twenty years ago, a new leader arose among the Assassins. His name was Rashideddin Sinan, and he decided to take things one step further. Starting with the already trained Fida'l, he started making cyborgs."

McGuire said, "Cyborg assassins?"

Jason nodded. "Oh yeah, and very nasty customers they are. The two I took out in the Moderator's Mansion were definitely cyborgs. Their bones had been replaced with very tough synthetic composites, and even their skulls were bulletproof. That's how they got by the Moderator's Bodyguard detail. Their whole body is basically armored, and they're impervious to most hand weapons."

Roland was professionally interested. "How'd you take them out?"

"Their eyes are vulnerable, and you can break their necks, although it was a lot harder than usual. Once the brain is out of play, they're just as dead as anyone else."

Roland nodded.

"Good to know." He turned to McGuire. "So what's the mission?"

Mcguire replied, "Insure that this does not happen again. We'd like to know who paid these guys, but if you can take out the source of the threat, that would be the main point of the exercise."

Roland nodded and looked over at Gillian. "Okay. We can do this, but it will only work if I lead the team."

She looked like she wanted to disagree, but she slowly nodded.

“And I’m going too,” said Jason.

Roland looked at him quizzically. “Patriotism? They can take the boy out of the Marine Corps, but they can’t take the Marine Corps out of the boy?”

Jason gave a thin smile. “They tried to kill Kristin too.”

“Got it. We certainly can’t have that. You’re in.”

## Chapter 6: Forebearers

"Richard," asked Kat, "how would you like to go out and see some Forebearer ruins?"

He looked over at her quizzically.

"They have ruins here on Achaea? I hadn't heard that." He gave her a mischievous smile. "Other than the neighborhood my dojo is in, of course."

She punched him in the shoulder and said, "Actually, I gather that there's an ongoing project to excavate the ruins they've found here. There's supposed to be something special or unusual about them."

Sure. Let's go."

Two hours later, Kat's aircar was banking over a pretty large excavation of what looked to Richard like a haphazard jumble of stones. This wasn't exactly surprising, given the timeframe that the Forebearers had flourished in.

It was really the Confederation press who had dubbed the beings that built these places the "Forebearers," not the archaeologists who had studied them. Ruined cities had been discovered on various planets throughout Confederation space. The ruins were always on Earth-like planets, but they had been dated at over a million years in the past. Speculation, of course, had been rife, and some science fiction authors had even decided that the Forebearers had been the ones who "tinkered" with hominids on Old Earth to cause them to evolve into modern humans. Some even believed that they were the gods of ancient Terra or the source of humanity itself.

As to what they had looked like, no one really knew. The ruins resided on planets with climates mostly like Old Earth, so they'd been eroded and worn down over the millennia to the point that only an expert could identify them as something built by sentient beings.

Kat came down in a slow spiral maneuver that brought them to an area where other vehicles were already parked. Given Kat's normal way of simulating a combat insertion even when she was at the controls of a civilian aircar, this landing was very sedate, in Richard's experience.

As they exited the vehicle, a young man in dust-covered khakis came up, a bit breathlessly. He froze for a moment, first getting a good look at Kat and then noticing Richard's robe. Shaking his head minutely, he said, "Ma'am, might you be Katerina Dunvegan?"

She smiled at the young man, which made him wriggle like a puppy that was having his tummy rubbed. Kat had that effect on some men.

She said, “Yes, I am, but most people just call me Kat.” She hooked her head at Richard. “And this is my friend, Richard Hawke.”

The kid nodded. “Sir, Ma’am. My name is Robert Guillaume. I’m one of Professor Grant Brummett’s students. If you’ll follow me, I think Professor Brummett can spare you some time for questions.”

“Thank you,” Kat said, “lead on.”

There was a large tent on the perimeter of the ruins, and Robert led them inside. Given that the excavation was in the middle of a desert area, the coolness inside the tent was very welcome to the two visitors.

Professor Brummett was middle-aged, around one hundred years old or so, in Michael’s estimation. He had grey hair thinning on the top. This in itself indicated that he wasn’t too concerned with personal appearances, because he could have had that corrected fairly easily. Perhaps he was cultivating the professorial look. The man had a round, deeply weathered face and piercing blue eyes, which he now turned on his guests.

The moment his eyes lighted on Kat, those eyes began to sparkle, and a large smile appeared on his face. As with the student earlier, Kat had that effect on a lot of men.

Including me, Richard thought.

The archaeologist shook both their hands, and they sat around a temporary table over in the corner of the room, obviously intended for beverage and meal breaks. The rest of the surfaces in the tent were covered in various pieces of what looked to Richard to be different sizes of rock, but were presumably artifacts of some sort. There were also various work stations, tablets, and at least one ongoing holo presentation being run in the corner by an earnest-looking young woman. Maybe she was editing it for public viewing or a press release. Or her homework, for that matter. She looked young enough to still be in school.

"May I ask what your level of interest is in this Miz Dunvegan?"

Ah, Richard thought, the scientist had picked up on Kat's family connections. Of course, he didn't know she was pretty much not on speaking terms with her father, the megalo-billionaire, or her brother, the Confederation Senator. He'd also apparently never heard of House Hawke, which Richard figured was just as well.

Kat gave one of her billion-watt smiles and replied, "Richard and I—" she nodded at Richard, and he nodded back, pleased that she had made the point that they were in this together. "—are both interested in history and archaeology, even though our respective lives have not allowed us to investigate such things directly."

Well, that was certainly true. Until pretty recently, Richard had been a monk in a Zen monastery and Kat had been a Navy fighter pilot. Winged comets of gold and all that.

Kat went on, "We had hoped that maybe we could get a mini-tour, without disturbing your work too much. I think that what you're doing here is too important."

Richard thought she was laying it on a little thick, but the professor clearly loved it. Maybe he didn't get a lot of people who thought his work was important. As far as Richard was concerned, Temujin Hawke had always said, "If we don't study history, we are doomed to repeat it."

Something had ended the reign of the Forebearers. It would be interesting to find out what that "something" had been, just in case there could be a repeat performance.

"Please come with me," said the archaeologist. They arose and followed him as he walked out through the open walls of the tent toward the excavation proper. Richard could see a number of people on the far end of a large, terraced hole. They appeared to be digging with small trowels, dental picks, and even small brushes. Zen is all about patience, but the scion of House Hawke didn't think he'd ever have enough interest in ancient civilizations to do that kind of work. Having said that, he was quite interested in the results of such research.

They negotiated a ladder to a lower level, and Brummett led them to a low wall of shapeless stones. Gesturing at them, he said, "This place hasn't been occupied in over a one hundred thousand years, possibly as much as a million. These people built to last, but that much time will reduce just about anything."

Kat said, "You refer to them as 'people.' Do you think they were human?"

He chuckled. "That is the million credit question. But to give you a proper answer, I believe that they were humanoid at least. What we have recovered of their buildings would be comfortable for a Terran human. To add to that, they built in ways similar to the most ancient civilizations on Old Earth."

Richard asked, "So do you believe that they visited Old Earth millennia ago, or even seeded Man-home as some believe?"

The professor shook his head. "We just don't have enough evidence to confirm either theory. In fact, that's the sort of lead we're hoping for here. This is one of the most recent cities that we've discovered. Recent in the sense that its demise was closer to human history than the others that have been found on other planets."

Kat asked, "Have you ever found any artifacts? Anything other than stone, for example?"

He gave her a small smile.

"God, I wish we had! That would silence the naysayers and kooks, at least." He gestured towards the tent. "C'mon, let's get in out of the sun."

He headed off and the visitors followed.

Richard asked, "Naysayers and kooks? I thought it was pretty established that the Forebearers existed, and that they had left all these ruins on multiple planets."

Professor Brummett gave a short laugh over his shoulder. "We should be so lucky! No, some of the religious freaks insist that God only created Man on Earth, and that beings on other planets could not have been created by God and must therefore be demons. They also deny that any of these ruins we've discovered were made by intelligent beings."

Kat's brow wrinkled. "But those two ideas don't make sense together. They would seem to be mutually exclusive. I've never heard of demons building anything in any scripture I've ever read."

The professor shook his head.

"I didn't say it was particularly logical. But then, quite a bit of religion is innately illogical." He chuckled. "And on the subject of religion, there are those who consider themselves scientists who also refuse to admit that the Forebearers ever existed."

It was Richard's turn to be puzzled. "But then where did these ruins come from?"

Brummett replied, "They say that these ruins are natural formations that just happen to resemble buildings, just like they said about the Bimini Road on Old Earth and the pyramids on Mars."

Kat said, "But we know those were built by that civilization that predated Ancient Egypt. What was it? Oh yeah, Aedan!"

The archaeologist waved his hand dismissively.

"Natural formations." He stopped and turned to look at them. "You see, some people get a model of the world into their heads that they will adamantly refuse to change, no matter how much evidence you throw at them. Come on. Let's head back."

As the three re-entered the open-air tent, three men came in from the opposite side. Richard immediately noted that all three were armed. He also noted that they were roughly dressed, more like factory workers than archaeologists. Two held slug pistols, while the other actually carried a plasma rifle.

A corner of Richard's mind wondered why they still called it a rifle, since the weapon didn't require any actual rifling, shooting a bolt of pure energy like it did.

Whatever you called it; it was a long gun and had a lot more range than the pistols. A person wouldn't want to brace anyone with a weapon like that from across some significant distance. You'd want to be closer, a lot closer.

Richard felt a feeling of peace and calm flowing through his body and spirit. He'd been trained so thoroughly that he didn't even have to think about this part. His respiration deepened, and oxygen flooded his system. Time seemed to slow around him.

As they approached the three men, the young woman who had been working on the holo presentation stood up. She clearly hadn't seen the men enter. Nor did it appear that she had realized that they carried weapons, or maybe she didn't see that as a real threat.

She said, "What are you people doing here?"

The man with the plasma rifle said, "Shut up, infidel bitch!"

With that, he hit her in the head with a horizontal butt stroke. The young woman fell, unconscious and bleeding.

While this was going on, Professor Brummett, Richard, and Kat had continued to walk in their direction. At ten feet, a whole lot closer than Richard would have allowed them, the man with the plasma rifle waved it in their direction and shouted, "Stop right there!"

The three stopped, and Brummett said in a mild voice, "Who are you people? And what do you want here?"

Plasma Rifle Dude and Scumbag One and Two, as Richard dubbed the pistoleros to his left and right, clearly felt that they were in charge of the situation. That was all to the good.

Plasma Rifle Dude said, "You people are unbelieving scum, trying to set these supposed Forebearers up as gods. There's only one God, and he created Man in his image!"

Richard looked over at Kat, and nodded. The two of them began to spread out from Brummett, very slowly.

The professor looked puzzled. "We're not trying to make the Forebearers out as gods. Far from it. We just want to find out about them; when they lived, and how they died."

The gunman stabbed the rifle at the archaeologist and screamed, "Liar!"

Kat stepped forward and thrust out her chest a bit. Suddenly, the pistol wielder directly in front of her was looking at her very intently. So was Scumbag Two.

Plasma Rifle must have caught something out of the corner of his eye, because his head swiveled in her direction as well.

With the bad guys' attention momentarily elsewhere, Richard launched an extended side kick at Scumbag Two. His hard heel smashed into the man's solar plexus, and the man was catapulted backwards out of the tent, losing his pistol as he went, a look of astonishment on his face.

Now Richard was next to Mister Plasma Rifle, and he flipped an iron-hard ridge hand into the man's eyes. Plasma Rifle yelled in pain, and Richard stepped in and both drove the man's weapon upwards and pulled him over his hip. A hip drag. Cool. If only his students were here to see it.

Scumbag One had realized that things were not going according to plan, and he began to turn his pistol toward Richard. It was at this point that Kat hit him over the head with a priceless Forebearer relic. A stone relic. A big stone relic. Hard. The man dropped, senseless.

Hawke immediately pivoted to return his attention to Scumbag Two, who was just getting to his feet. Richard snap kicked him in the face, and the man went over backwards, unconscious.

"Bastards!" said Plasma Rifle Dude as he tried to bring his rifle to bear. Drawing a bead on Kat, he fired.

Kat had seen the weapon heading in her direction, and with her fighter pilot's reflexes, she threw herself down and to the side. The plasma bolt flashed by her head as she rolled to the side to keep the man from getting a bead on her.

With a piercing Kiai spirit shout, Richard, brought the edge of his hand down on the man's neck. The neck snapped, and Plasma Rifle Dude dropped face down, dead.

Richard immediately went to Kat's side. He knelt next to her as she came up on her hands and knees.

He said, "Are you all right?"

Kat grinned and replied, "I am now." She looked around. "Is everybody else all right?"

Professor Brummett was looking past her, his eyes wide.

Richard and Kat looked in the same direction, half expecting to see another casualty, but what they saw instead was a hole in the side of the mountain. An apparently very deep hole.

Richard said, "I guess that's where the plasma bolt hit."

Brummett rushed over to the hole. "It's a hidden chamber! And I think there are artifacts inside!"

"Cool!" was all Richard had to say.

# Chapter 7: Follow the Leader

Old Earth was not an enormously populous place these days. The bulk of human population had moved toward the center of the Galaxy, to places like Starcastle, where there were more opportunities. Earth, or Terra if you preferred the more formal name, was pretty laid back. Its main income was from tourist credits, and the rich and famous who liked to sample the quaint backwater that was Man-home.

All of this made it much easier for Koo to track the guy who'd tried to have them killed. He'd set out on one of the jet-bikes from their garage. That way, the ground-effect Mercedes wouldn't be able to lose him by going off-road, no matter how unlikely that might be in a luxury car. In any kind of straight race, the bike could keep up with them.

Cuchulain was not raised by fools, of course, so he kept his distance. The other guys must know by this time that their hit team was toast, so they might be watching for a tail. With this sort of thing in mind, the bike was partially stealthed, so it would not be obvious to most sensor suites. It could, of course be picked up visually if he got too close, so Koo laid back and let the tracer do its job.

"We're coming into Denver," he said.

"I know," his father said, "I've got you on my HUD."

"On your HUD? Aren't you back at the house?"

"No, I'm in the recon flitter, about five miles above and behind you."

The recon flitter was full-stealth, invisible to radar, lidar, IR, and visual. It was essentially invisible to all sensors. All that was well and good, but Koo had thought he was handling this by himself.

"Koo," Temujin said, knowing exactly what his son was thinking, "I trust you completely. But I want in on this. This idiot tried to attack the House Hawke. I want to be along to teach him the error of his ways."

The Mercedes pulled into an underground parking garage in downtown Denver. Koo would have been surprised if the guy he was tailing had headed anywhere else. Although Denver wasn't a spaceport, it was the largest city in the area, and it had connections to all the major cities worldwide, as well as the various spaceports.

Cuchulain quickly parked his bike nearby. He didn't want to be picked up going into the building, and exfiltration might be easier if he was able to just walk out of the building. That would be especially true if anything went down inside. Of course, Dad always stressed a virtually invisible insertion and exit, but Koo had learned to prepare for those events which followed the laws promulgated by that ancient sage, Murphy. If things could go wrong, they probably would. Best to have a fallback plan. Or two.

There was a security guard in a kiosk at the entrance. Sauntering casually towards the door of the garage, Koo flipped a marble across to the other side of the entrance. The security guard's head whipped around toward the sound, and Koo ghosted into the garage behind him. Quickly moving into some nearby shadows, the young man looked around for the Mercedes he'd been shadowing.

There it was near the lift tubes, and his quarry was just entering the lifts, along with another man in a chauffeur's uniform.

Moving so fast, he was almost a blur, the young Hawke ran over to the lifts. He summoned a tube of his own, all the time watching the floor indicator on the lift the target had taken. The penthouse. No big surprise. Koo punched in the one hundred and fiftieth floor, just below the penthouse level. The lift rose smoothly.

Exiting the lift casually, the young Hawke quickly moved to the stairwell at the end of the hallway. Taking the plastcrete stairs up one floor, he reached the penthouse level. The emergency door to the penthouse was locked, but he drew a tanto from between his shoulder blades, and cut through the lock with one swift slice. Battle steel was used in the armor for spacegoing dreadnoughts, and the battle steel edge of Koo's blade was more than a match for even the hardest civilian alloys.

There was a slight "ting" as the metal of the lock parted, and Koo waited for a moment to see if that got any reaction. When no one burst through the door to kill him, he moved through the door into a lush suite of rooms. This penthouse occupied the entire floor, so he had entered directly into the enemy's lair. He re-sheathed the knife. Although the Hawke clan was conversant with most types of weapons, and expert in the use of many of them, they were trained not to rely on them totally. Too often, situations could change suddenly, and it was best to not put all your focus on one type of attack. The most dangerous weapon that Cuchulain Hawke had at his disposal was—himself. Empty hand techniques were looked upon with disdain by most soldiers and killers. The Hawkes knew better. The human body was more deadly than the most powerful plasma weapon. Having said that, range could pose a problem, but that was the point of practice.

He heard voices from the next room, so he moved in that direction. Opening the door slowly and carefully, the Hawke took in the entirety of the room. There was the guy he'd followed, engaged in an animated conversation with someone on a holophone. To Koo's right, the driver of the Mercedes was having a sandwich at a dinette center. To his left, a beefy bodyguard type was lounging on an expensive looking couch, playing with a huge Bowie-style knife. Cuchulain wondered if the rule about the size of the knife being in inverse proportion to penis size applied here. Probably.

The target was saying, "Hawke refused, Mister Petrov, so I activated the extermination order. By this time, he should be safely dead. And yes, his family too."

So maybe he didn't know his hit team was already dead. Cool!

Moving quickly but silently, Koo entered the room. He was within five feet of the bodyguard before the man noticed him, and by that time, it was too late. One hand sliced across the man's eyes, blinding him, and a half fist crushed his throat. Koo grabbed the huge fighting knife out of the strangling man's hands, pivoted, and threw it across the room. The chauffeur had just stood up in alarm when the force of the blade slammed him back against a wooden cabinet. The knife was long enough that it pinned him to the cabinet wall. He tried to say something, but blood gushed from his mouth.

Koo went airborne across the room. Normally, flying kicks were contraindicated, because they left the kicker so wide open and helpless to counters, but in this case, speed was of the essence. The hard edge of his heel took the man at the phone in the spine. There was a nasty crunching sound, and the man dropped to the floor with a cry. Koo landed, regained his balance, and checked the room for any other threats. All targets had been serviced.

He walked to the phone, and looked at the overweight, balding man at the other end. Koo quickly slapped a tracer on the phone unit, and then looked into the image and smiled.

"Hello, Mister Petrov. My name is Hawke, and I'll be seeing you soon." Looking down, he saw the call had been tracked, so he cut the connection.

The man from the Mercedes was crying in pain. He said, "I can't move my legs! I can't move my legs!"

Koo looked down at him.

"You tried to kill me and my family. But I want you to take a message for me. Don't fuck with the Hawkes." He started to turn away, but then turned back. "On second thought, never mind. I'll be delivering the message myself."

The edge of Hawke's boot hit the man in the temple, killing him instantly.

# Chapter 8: Mission Statement

"So what are the mission parameters?" Roland Hawke asked.

The Central Intelligence weenie nodded. Clearly, he had expected the question. "We want you to neutralize the threat."

Jason gave a sour laugh. "So you want the assassins dead. I get that, and I heartily agree. But what about their paymasters and the guys who are controlling them?"

"We do not want this threat to arise again."

Roland nodded.

"Okay, kill them all, root and branch." He looked over at Gillian. "That might require special resources, if we're going to pay a visit to the Old Man on Alamut."

She looked at the CI rep. "My understanding is that we can use any assets we need, and that all expenses will be covered."

The government man nodded. "That is correct."

Roland said, "But, of course, if we're caught, you've never heard of us."

Jason laughed. "As usual, when you're dealing with the government."

The CI guy chose not to comment.

"All right," said Ms. Straley, "what have you got in the way of information for us?"

He handed her a data marble.

"Here's all we've got." He stood. "And with that, I must get back to the office."

The man nodded to the three of them and left.

Once the door had closed, Roland said, "And that may or may not actually be all they have on Alamut."

He turned to Jason. "I remember a bit about the Hashishiyun, but not a whole lot. For one thing, I had no idea that they were employing cyborgs."

Jason nodded. "Voluntary cyborgs, at that, I believe. The guys that attacked the Moderator were very tough. They had some sort of non-metallic sub-epidermal armor. The Bodyguards shot them multiple times center mass, and it didn't even slow them down. One guard did kill one when he shot him in the eye, and I was able to take two out by removing their brain stem from their brains."

Roland nodded. As though he had been there, he could see what his brother had done. They had the same training, after all. For Gillian's sake, he said, "So you broke their necks. It's a chink in their armor, anyway. I guess they must have needed the mobility for their heads, or they would have armored their necks, too."

Jason said, "Yeah." He raised his right hand. "My hand is still kind of swollen from hitting one in the head. Autopsies found that their skulls were armored too."

Roland said, "So guns will work, but you'd better be a really good shot."

Jason agreed. "Same with blades. The good news is that these guys seemed kind of overconfident. I can kind of see that, but they never ran into a Hawke before."

Gillian added, "Well, we'd better hit them soon, before they process that data and come up with better defenses."

"Agreed."

"Agreed."

Roland said, "Okay, Bro, I've got some things to arrange. Get your things together. I can comm you at home?"

"Correctomundo. I take it you'll handle the hardware?"

"Whatever we need will be loaded on the ship."

"Good. I'll have to talk to Kristin, although she already knows that I'm committed to this."

"Well, good luck with that."

* * * *

"I don't want you to go," said Kristin Baird.

Jason was packing a few things, including various knives and a pair of swords. He knew that Roland would have a good selection of guns, but Jason thought that things might get in close, and he wanted his own blades.

Over his shoulder, he said, "You know I've got to go." He turned to face her. "Those Green geeks didn't care who was with the Moderator. They were going to kill anyone there. I'm not going to let that happen." He held up a hand to forestall the retort that he knew was coming. "Hey, I know you might not be there the next time they come calling. But somebody else will be, and the next time, I won't be there to stop them."

"Oh you bastard!" she cried as she flung herself into his arms. She sobbed for a minute. Then she looked up at him and said, "Okay, I know that you feel you have to go. But if you get killed, I'll never speak to you again!"

He gave her a gentle smile. "Well, I'd better make sure I don't get killed then."

* * * *

"I'd really rather you didn't have to go on this one," said Gillian, in Roland's arms.

He nodded. "It's what I do, though." He grinned. "At least until I become an exalted upper executive like yourself."

She smacked his arm and stepped back. "You're head of Galactica's Special Operations Section now. You could assign someone else to this mission."

He shook his head.

"No. There's really no one else in the section that has my level of training and expertise in something like this. If I assigned somebody else, they'd probably just get themselves killed." He spread his hands dramatically. "I, on the other hand, will succeed in the mission, make the company a lot of money, and get an excellent performance review."

She couldn't help but smile. "Try not to be so humble. It doesn't suit you."

"Okay, but humble or not, I need to pack."

He started to turn away, but she grabbed him by the ears and kissed him soundly. "You come back to me, you hear?"

"Will do, Ma'am!" He kissed her back.

* * * *

"Scotty, how are things coming?" Roland called from the ship's ramp.

The pilot, Scott Douglas, came walking from the bow wiping his hands on an oily rag. "Hi, Mister Hawke. Things are coming right along. I should be done loading the supplies by tonight."

Roland said, "And that includes the 'special supplies'?"

Smitty nodded. "If by special you mean that buttload of guns and ammo, then yes. They're all already on board in Number Two hold."

"Good. My brother Jason will be coming along on this one."

"And will that pretty Kat Dunvegan be shipping out with us too? She's one hell of a backup pilot."

Roland smiled. "Not this time, I'm afraid. Kat and my brother Richard are off touring the Border worlds, no doubt having a fine old time."

* * * *

Raising herself up on one elbow, the sheet strategically draped over various parts of her body, Kat asked, "So, Mister Hawke, how would you like to visit an ASP boat base?"

He looked at her quizzically. "An ASP boat base? They have one of those here on Achaea?"

She nodded. "Yep. Anti-Ship Patrol boats are a fairly new design idea. They're bigger than a fighter. They have a crew of five. But I guess they pack one hell of a wallop, with some big torpedoes and one decent-sized energy cannon."

Richard dropped his robe over his head. Emerging from the folds, he said, "So what are these things for? I mean, the Confederation Navy has lots of bigger ships, and the fighters are small and fast."

Kat stood up, leaving the sheet behind, and walked naked to the closet. As she sorted through her clothes, she cast a sly eye over at Richard to see if he was paying attention. Satisfied that he was, she said, "The ASP boats are seen as a reasonably inexpensive way to defend the border systems."

She pulled on a short silk robe. “The Navy can’t be everywhere, and ships of the line are extremely pricey. The ASP boats are big enough to slow an enemy down, and maybe tough enough to cause damage that will stop him cold.”

Richard nodded. “So do you agree with that theory?”

She shrugged, which did interesting things to the silk robe.

“It’s never been tested. Right now, it’s just that, a theory.” She paused. “That’s why I’d like to see them.”

“To form your own opinions?”

“Of course. What could be more fun and romantic than to visit a ASP boat base out here on the fringe of civilization?”

He grinned. “Sure. Fun.”

“And romantic. Don’t forget romantic.”

He smiled. “Around you, how could I forget the romantic part?”

# Chapter 9: Developments

Roland and Jason Hawke were sitting at a workstation in Galactica Security's offices at Starcastle. They'd been reviewing the data given to them by Central Intelligence.

Jason looked sour. "This sucks, as usual. This is about as much information as we used to get before a mission. It's just a hundred-thousand-foot overview, with very little useful information for the grunt on the ground!"

"Well, it does give us a couple of leads. The intel weenies found out that the actual assassins, your boys in green, came in on a Nihon spaceliner, the Nagata Maru."

Jason responded, "And we already know that they ultimately came from Alamut."

Roland nodded. "True. But our mission parameters say to eliminate the threat completely. Sure, we could probably take out the people giving the orders, but there could be the odd Hashishiyun wandering around, still on a mission to kill people in the Confederation."

Jason nodded grudgingly. "Okay, I get it. So where to?"

Roland was still reading through the intel take. He said, "I think we need to head to Osaka. It's one of the Nihon worlds. We should be able to backtrack these guys farther from there."

"And if they have paymasters or controls there, we can question them."

Roland added, "And then terminate them."

Jason agreed. "Kill them all. A lot."

* * * *

"Dad," Koo said into the encrypted holophone, "I've booked passage on a spaceliner to New London."

Temujin's face remained impassive. "I take it that you've tracked the lovely and talented Mister Petrov there?"

"Yes, Sir. I want to follow up on him as quickly as possible. Since his call with that local dude was on an FTL comm link, he might decide to vacate the premises if he thinks I'm coming to talk to him."

His father nodded. "Maybe, and that's good thinking, but I suspect he'll still be there. Two-bit bosses like him think they're untouchable. He'll think you'd be nuts to come after him."

Koo smiled.

"Well, I plan on touching him, hard." Just then, there was a boarding announcement, and Koo saw a really cute blond heading toward the entrance for his shuttle. "See you, Dad. I've got to get going."

He discommed abruptly, which might piss off his father, but he'd have time to get over it, and that blond was really cute!

Ten minutes later, and thanks to a significant gratuity, Cuchulain Hawke was seated next to the attractive blond he'd seen in the terminal.

"Hi!" he opened brightly, "My name is Koo Williams."

He had papers for multiple personalities, but the Williams persona appealed to him. The family had a distant ancestor by that name. Off the top of his head, he couldn't remember the guy's first name. Romeo or something like that. Apparently, he'd been one heck of an assassin, though.

The woman smiled, somewhat reluctantly he thought, but she offered her hand and replied, "Hello. My name is Gemma Jackson. You can call me Gem."

He thought that the name fit. She was indeed a real gem. But in a momentary lapse of pure wisdom, he decided to keep that particular comment to himself. Instead, he said, "Well, my real name is Cuchulain, but everybody calls me Koo. Cuchulain is a little bit of a jawbreaker."

She wrinkled her brow in what Koo thought was a thoroughly charming manner and said, “Is that a name from New Wales?”

He laughed. “I wish. No it’s an old Irish name from right here on Old Earth. You were close, though. Both the Irish and the Welsh are of Celtic origins.”

She nodded. “It’s good to know your roots.”

He gave her a wide smile.

“Oh, our family goes way, way back.” Which was true enough. They had a long history of successful assassinations. “How about your family?”

Gem wrinkled her nose. “Oh, nothing special. My family were minor bureaucrats on Starcastle. That’s where I grew up.”

He raised his eyebrows. “And did you become a minor bureaucrat too?”

She shook her head, smiling slightly. “Oh not me. I got a job as an investigator.”

“That sounds like it could be exciting. My family tends to specialize in account adjusting. You know, if somebody has been cooking the books, we get tasked to correct any imbalances. We’re sort of accountants.” That was his Dad’s favorite inside joke and cover. And it was true in a way. The Hawkes adjusted accounts and restored balance to the system, with extreme prejudice.

Koo was looking forward to the upcoming trip with more and more enthusiasm.

* * * *

Kat's credentials and a letter of introduction got them onto the Confederation Navy base on Achaea. Even to Richard's unmilitary eye, the place looked kind of small and run down.

They came to a stop in front of a prefab building with a sign out front:

*HOME OF ANTI-SHIP PATROL BOAT SQUADRON 10:*

*Fast In, Fast Out!*

Richard said, "I assume that they're referring to their boats."

Kat laughed. "Never assume. These guys are Navy."

He nodded sagely. "Oh, of course. What was I thinking?"

They went inside. There was a middle-aged Chief Petty Officer sitting at a desk that faced the door. Several open office doors were across the room from him, and they could see what appeared to be a fairly large conference or briefing room directly ahead.

Kat walked directly to the CPO and said, "Chief, I'm Katerina Dunvegan. I have an appointment with Lieutenant Commander James Lewis."

He looked at her for a moment, and then stood up, almost at a position of attention. "Oh, Captain Dunvegan! We're very glad to have you here!" The chief gave Richard a questioning look, and then said to Kat, "I'll get the Lieutenant Commander for you, Ma'am."

He walked briskly off down the line of offices and disappeared from sight.

Richard looked gravely at Kat. "I don't think he's too sure what to make of me. But I gather he knows exactly who you are."

She smiled. "Well, if you're going to be famous, you might as well put that to work for you."

"And you are somewhat famous for our exploits, particularly in the naval community."

She nodded. "Exactly. But don't forget the family name. That can be influential at times as well."

The chief came back in a few seconds with a fairly young officer in tow. The lieutenant commander was tall and slim, with a wiry strength inherent in his frame. He had blond hair and bright blue eyes that radiated intelligence.

The officer came straight to Kat and stuck out his hand. "Captain Katerina Dunvegan! It's a real pleasure to meet you. I knew of your combat successes during the war on Taegu, and then I saw both the newsfaxes and the official reports about what you did on Bishti. I'm most impressed!"

The young officer was positively beaming. Behind him, the chief petty officer rolled his eyes a bit. Clearly, he was used to his commander's enthusiasms.

Kat gave the officer a smile and gestured to Richard. "And this is my friend, Richard Hawke. He was my backseater when we did our thing on Bishti."

A look of dawning respect shone on the faces of both the commanding officer and his chief. The commander said, “And I don’t know if he’s introduced himself, but this is Chief Petty Officer Jim Wilson. Other than our most senior Chief, he’s also sitting in as our Engineering Officer. When it comes to spacecraft, Jim knows everything about everything. He’s the one that really keeps this lash-up going.”

Kat smiled and shook the enlisted man’s hand. She said, “Good to meet you, Chief. God knows, without our ground crew, we would have been absolutely toast on Taegu.”

Wilson actually blushed. “Thank you, Captain Dunvegan.”

The lieutenant commander grabbed a cover from a hat tree near the door. “Come on. I’ll show you around.”

A few minutes later, Lewis gestured at the blasted cement of the spaceport before them and said, “And here are our babies.”

There were about a dozen ships in the open or in revetments across the landing field. To Richard’s untrained eye, they looked quite large, but then he thought about it. He’d seen fighter spacecraft, and these boats were about three times bigger than them. And he’d been on some pretty large naval vessels, destroyers up to battleships, and these craft were way smaller than those.

“So unlike their battleship brethren, these ASPs are small enough to land on a planet?” he asked.

Commander Lewis smiled and replied, “An astute question, Mister Hawke. I believe that you have both seen the Celestia? Good. The Celestia is extremely unusual in that it's a large spacecraft that can actually land on hard dirt." He stamped on the concrete walkway for emphasis. "Other large spacecraft are built in space and live only in space. You need shuttles to get to them. On the other hand, we have fighters, which can easily land on either planets of carriers in space. Now, I grant you, there are some small yachts that can also take off or land planetside, but by and large naval vessels cannot."

He gestured at the boats again. "This is a tradeoff. Our craft are just small enough that, with a full cargo of weapons, crew, and reaction mass, these boats can land planetside. It makes resupply and maintenance way easier, and we can take on seawater from the bay over there as reaction mass. It's a win-win situation."

"How about their armament?" asked Kat, looking the boats over with a professional eye.

"Ah yes, the armament. These babies carry eight Tigershark space torpedoes, large enough to take out much larger ships up to and including destroyers." He paused to let them take that in. "But our real mission in a hot war would be commerce raiding, destroying cargo vessels. Deprive the enemy of supplies, and he will wither on the vine."

The boats were roughly cylindrical, with stubby delta wings sticking out of their sides and a large vertical stabilizer on the tail. Positioned geometrically around their sides were long blisters that Richard guessed housed the torpedoes. Clearly, there wasn't room for more than the eight missiles. Once the torpedoes were spent, the little vessels would have only short range energy weapons. That would be okay for cargo ships, but for vessels of war?

Kat looked at the squadron commander. "So if enemy cruisers show up, you and your guys beat feet?"

Lewis smiled. "Absolutely. Anything else would be suicide. Not only that, but the Achaeans have their own navy, albeit a small one. They shouldn't really need us."

"What sort of fleet does a place like this have?" asked Kat.

Lewis gave a sheepish grin. "Well, not a great one, I'll admit. They have two twenty-year-old destroyers and a cruiser that was in service in my grandfather's time." He brightened. "Still they have quite a bit of practical experience in operations against pirates, and they can use their equipment to the best of its ability."

Richard and Kat exchanged glances. Neither of them would want to be here if a real Desotoan fleet showed up in the ecliptic.

# Chapter 10: Movements

"Admiral, I'm getting reports of Desotoan fleet movement all along the border of the Antilles Sector," said Captain Joe Fuchida, Third Fleet's intelligence chief.

Admiral Ghormley, the fleet's commander, made a "come on" gesture for the officer to continue.

"I know that the Desotoans said that they were going to have fleet exercises in that general area, but they're operating a whole lot closer to our border than anyone anticipated. It wouldn't take anything for them to infringe on Confederation space near Antilles, and we don't have a whole lot of assets in that area."

Ghormley looked thoughtful for long minutes. It was obvious that his brain was working furiously.

"This could be feint to draw us out of position, but I don't think we can safely ignore it, especially after that business off Bishti. We bloodied their nose pretty well that time, but I'd have been astonished if it had caused them to just give up." He stood and went over to the holo-globe of a star chart and studied it for a few seconds. "Frankly, I'm surprised it's taken this long for them to become active again." He turned back. "Okay, have my chief of staff get in here, and have my aide arrange a meeting of the unit commanders. We're going to have to go show the flag in the Antilles Sector, I'm afraid."

"Aye-aye, Sir!"

"Oh, and send my aide in here, too. I'm going to have to inform Starcastle that things are starting to get interesting out here."

About a minute later, Lieutenant George Prochnow entered Admiral Ghormley's office. "You needed me, Admiral?"

Ghormley studied his aide de camp for a moment. He hadn't told Prochnow this, but he was about to be promoted out of his job. He'd done an excellent job as aide, but it was time for him to move on to a command of his own. From Prochnow's perspective, the last few years had been an invaluable look into the behind-the-scenes running of a Confederation Star Fleet. It was also clear that he idolized his boss, which the Admiral understood could come with the territory. Ghormley himself had served commanders whose major lesson to him had been how not to do things once he had a command of his own. He hoped he'd done a better job than that for his own aide.

"George," Ghormley began, "get your grammar cap on. Joe Fuchida has pretty solid information that the Desotoans are going to be 'exercising' their fleet near our border with them in the Antilles Sector. Draft a message to Fleet at Starcastle for my approval that we're moving Third Fleet to Antilles. We'll leave a fighter squadron at Achaea, along with those damned useless ASPs. Maybe the Achaeans can see some way to make them useful."

"Aye-aye, Sir!" Prochnow said with a grin. He knew that the admiral thought that the whole Anti-Ship Patrol boat concept was a waste of time and money. Prochnow wasn't so sure, but Admiral Ghormley generally knew what he was talking about.

* * * *

Don Juan de Balboa, the Sub-Director of the Foreign Intelligence Service for the Desotoan Empire, was contemplating the latest request he'd received from Admiral Julio Torres, the Chief of Naval Operations. The "request", if you could call it that, demanded that Foreign Intelligence send Torres all the information that they had on Achaea.

Balboa, a self-made man who had come up through the ranks by dint of hard work and brains, despised Torres, who was a purely political appointee. He also truly hated Rear Admiral Guillermo Garcia, the head of

Naval Intelligence. Balboa knew that both owed their positions to political patronage, and he considered them both idiots and aggressive control freaks. In addition to that, in Garcia's case, Balboa considered Naval Intelligence to be a competitor for governmental influence and funding. He felt that the Office of Naval Intelligence, if you could call it that, should be dissolved, and that the responsibility for all intelligence and covert operations should devolve to Foreign Intelligence. To Balboa, that only made sense, but the military services saw things differently, and so far they'd been able to retain their independence.

Unfortunately, the two Navy twits were very politically connected, so it could be very career-limiting for Balboa to simply ignore their requests. After that mess in the Bishti Sector, the former head of the intelligence services, Enrique Mendoza, had been demoted and disappeared. Balboa knew he had to tread lightly if he didn't want to share that fate. Emperor Fernando I de Aragon did not react well to failure or anything that might embarrass the Empire. Premier Ollarsaba was even less lenient.

But perhaps Balboa could limit the amount and nature of the intelligence he made available to the two Navy morons. If, for example, he didn't give them any of the raw data, but only sent evaluations, that would be good enough. Of course, professionalism wouldn't let him reveal his sources. And if those evaluations happened to be ones that were not only somewhat overly optimistic, but also happened to coincide with what the two idiot admirals wanted to believe anyway, well that would be all to the good. And if the Navy wound up with egg on its face over the whole affair, then, that would also be all to the good from Balboa's perspective, too. After all, he would be able to show that he'd provided them with the information they requested. It wasn't his fault that the bumbling fools didn't know what to do with it. And if they succeeded, then the Foreign Intelligence chief could justifiably claim that he was at least partially responsible for that success. No matter who won or who lost, Balboa and his Foreign Intelligence Service would come out of this looking good.

There was the minor matter of the assassins that the Imperial security Foreign Intelligence guys had employed, but he'd made sure that they were all third-party contractors. If they failed, he had several layers of plausible deniability. If they succeeded, and the star nations were looking for someone to hang, then Balboa was the invisible man. And success would also point up how supportive of the entire effort Foreign Intelligence had been. Again, no matter who won and who lost, Juan de Balboa came out smelling like a rose!

It would be ever so pleasant to pull funding from Naval Intelligence and have it reallocated to Balboa's own group. He smiled at the thought. The fact that men might die in the process was deplorable, but necessary for the greater good.

# Chapter 11: The Big Lie

Robes were not all that unusual on Achaea, and the two robed men who approached Government House in New Athens, the capital city of Achaea, were fairly nondescript. There was nothing in particular to distinguish them from anyone else. When they passed the detectors at the front portals, there were no alarms or indications that anything was amiss.

But an older guard, Demetrios Patroclus, a veteran of the security forces for many years, smelled something odd about the two. He held up a hand and said, "Gentlebeings, can I ask your business at Government House?"

He rested one hand on the shock baton at his belt as he spoke, and his eyes were sharp.

The two robed men looked at each other and smiled. The one to Patroclus' right, slightly taller, bowed to him and replied, "Our business is with your President."

The guard didn't move his hand from his shock baton. "What sort of business? And do you have an appointment?"

The man laughed. "We do not need an appointment. We do as our Master bids."

Demetrios pulled the baton and said, "All right. That's enough. Nikos! Alexandros! Remove these two from the premises."

The two younger guards approached the two interlopers, their faces serious. Suddenly, the man who had not spoken turned to face them. The two pulled off their robes in matching moves to reveal form-fitting green uniforms under them. With no warning, both men attacked.

Patroclus had time to strike the man coming at him once. He also had time to be shocked that the baton had absolutely no effect before the green-clad assassin crushed his skull with a smashing blow.

The murderer turned to see that his partner had killed both of the other guards.

"Good," he said, emotionlessly, "let us be about our mission."

* * * *

Kat and Richard were just shaking hands with Lieutenant Commander Lewis when three men with guns burst through the door.

Kat muttered, “Oh, not again!” She then threw herself to the floor behind Chief Petty Officer Wilson’s desk.

Commander Lewis said, “What do you people think you’re doing?”

At the same moment, the CPO drew a large-caliber pistol from beneath the desk.

Each of the three intruders carried a shoulder weapon, more suited to long-range targets, but certainly deadly at close range if necessary. One began to swing his weapon toward Wilson; another brought his weapon to bear on the ASP commander, while the third started to bring his own gun to bear on Richard.

The weapon never quite got pointed at Hawke. As soon as the weapons began to move to targets, he was moving. Robes can make movement deceptively fast, partly because it’s harder to see the feet move. Richard was on his gunman, and his left hand came up under the gun while his right half-fist lashed out, crushing the man’s throat. The man clutched his throat, and Richard took his weapon from him.

The middle gunman had fired at Commander Lewis, but, distracted by Richard’s attack, he missed and Lewis threw himself across the floor. As the attacker tried to bring his gun to bear on the erstwhile monk, Richard slapped the butt of the rifle he held into his right hand. He still held the barrel in his left, and he used the two-handed grip to deliver a horizontal butt stroke to the gunman’s temple. The man dropped.

A gun crashed, and the brains of the last attacker splashed across the room. Petty Officer Wilson had voiced his opinion of people breaking into his office and disturbing his afternoon coffee break.

Lewis stood back up as Kat also arose from her cover.

Lewis said, "What the hell was that all about?"

Kat said, "Commander, I think they were looking to take you out."

"Why the blazes would they want to do that?"

Richard added, "They may have been trying to take out the command structure of this squadron."

Shots were heard across the compound, and CPO Wilson said, "I think they're right Commander. And I don't think we're the only ones."

* * * *

One hour later, Kat, Richard, and Commander Lewis were listening to emergency broadcasts from all over Achaea.

Lewis' eyes remained glued to the holovision as he said, "So we're in the middle of a rebellion."

The local news agencies showed views of riots and armed confrontations in several of the major cities around the globe.

Kat said, "Interesting that they took out the President and the higher government heads first. That tells me that this has been planned for quite some time, and that the rebels have a lot of resources."

"If they really are rebels," said Richard Hawke.

The others looked at him. Lewis said, “What do you mean by that?”

Richard shook his head. “This is all too neat. Spontaneous global rebellion in a peaceful realm? And a realm, I might add, that borders directly on the De Soto Empire.” He paused. “I think it’s a contrived situation.”

Kat’s eyes had narrowed. “But to what end?”

Richard nodded at the holo.

“To create chaos, maybe even an incident.” He looked over at the commander. “Do the Desotoans have any large naval units in the vicinity?”

Lewis shook his head. “Not that I’m aware of. But I’m pretty low on the food chain here. I’m going to make some inquiries.”

Kat watched the on-screen violence. “Better safe than sorry.”

* * * *

Moderator James Brown looked up as his senior aide came into the office. “What’s up, Bob?”

Roberto Valdez took a data marble to the processor against the wall. “You’re going to want to see this, Sir.”

Brown replied in a dry tone, “Somehow, I doubt that.”

A picture of the Desotoan Foreign Secretary, Don Francisco Pizarro, appeared, and immediately began reading from what was obviously a prepared script. “Today, units associated with a popular rebellion in the system of our neighbor, Achaea, attacked the embassy and businesses of Desotoan nationals in the capital city of Achaea. Unrest there continues. The De Soto Empire has decided it must contain this violence and mitigate the danger to its citizens. To accomplish this, a squadron of Desotoan warships has been dispatched to the Achaean System, where they will evacuate any Desotoan citizens and quell any further violence, with deadly force if necessary."

The Moderator of the Confederation of Planets said, "Oh shit. Those bastards are trying to annex Achaea."

Valdez replied, "But they said that they were just trying to rescue their citizens."

Brown shook his head. "Yeah, and you can believe as much of that as you can stomach. Make no mistake; this is a grab for territory." He paused for a moment, and then said, "Get me Admiral Ghormley on the FTL. He's going to have to be ready for an attack."

* * * *

Chief Petty Officer Wilson came into Commander Lewis' office. Kat and Richard looked up as well. Wilson said, "Sir, we just got word. A Desotoan squadron just dropped out of warp in this system."

Lewis looked a bit punchy by this added disastrous news, but he asked, "Estimated strength?"

Wilson looked at a paper in his hands. "It looks like two cruisers and five tin cans, Commander."

Lewis just said, "Oh shit."

# Chapter 12: Elimination Round

Cuchulain Hawke exited the shuttle at New London on the planet of Winchester. It was with some reluctance that he'd left the new-found love of his life, Gemma Jackson, but she was continuing on to Eire. She'd told him that she had business there.

Once on the ground and in the city, Koo consulted a local directory for Nikolai Petrov, the paymaster of the hit team that had attacked the Hawke compound. Surprisingly, the name was readily available. Apparently, the scumbag was a pillar of the local community, with his fingers in many business pies. Dad had been right again. This guy was too arrogant to go to ground.

Whether Petrov was an agent or the ultimate boss, his office was in one of the higher-priced business sections of New London, and Koo grabbed a ground-effect bus to get himself there. Once in the neighborhood, he strolled around the area, reconnoitering the immediate environment and getting a feel for the kind of people who would be the most invisible.

In Temujin Hawke's curriculum for his sons, he had included some tenets on effective invisibility. Of course, military chamo outfits were the high tech option. They made the wearer literally invisible, essentially making a soldier (or assassin) blend with whatever environment they were closest too, through the use of high tech fibers and picotech.

However, there was an older and in some ways more effective method, especially in an urban area. This technique involved "uniforms". This did not mean a soldier's uniform necessarily, although it could. The idea was that people see what they expect to see. So if the spy or assassin wears the clothes of a maintenance man, or a policeman, or a priest, observers tend to only see the uniform. They don't look at, nor do they remember, the person. If a mission involved infiltrating a military compound, a military uniform might indeed be used. If the target is in a police station, the assassin might dress as a policeman. People tended to only see the priest, janitor, soldier, or policeman rather than an assassin, spy, or even the person wearing the "uniform."

Koo spent some time on his reconnaissance, noting what sort of people came and went. Most wore formal business attire, but there were a fair number of workman and delivery personnel as well. He decided to go with a maintenance worker. They could go just about anywhere, as long as they moved purposefully and looked like they had a job to do.

Fading into a nearby alley, Koo found just the sort of guy he was looking for. Koo left a pile of local currency under the unconscious man's head to cushion his painful awakening.

The youngest Hawke also stuffed some random paper and plastic under the shirt to give himself a bit of a belly and love handles. If Koo had a problem with disguise, it was that he was too good looking. Women tended to notice him no matter what he wore. He also rubbed a bit of dirt under his eyes to make himself look older and more tired. Finally, he covered his blond hair with a billed cap.

Entering the office building through the main entrance, he garnered few glances. The erstwhile maintenance man glanced casually at the holo directory for the building. He located Petrov Investments on the fiftieth floor. Next, he walked, just as casually, toward the rear of the building, figuring that would be where the freight lifts were. Some investigation revealed a stairwell that paralleled the lift tubes. That was good to know in case he needed an alternate method of egress. On the other hand, he had no need or desire to trudge up fifty floors on the stairs.

The freight lift dropped him on the forty-eighth floor. Now would be the time to take the stairs. With utmost care, he entered the stairwell and moved upwards. As he reached the landing for the forty-ninth floor, he heard a faint noise above him. Moments later, the faint aroma of a dopestick filtered down to the stealthy Hawke. It was very poor tradecraft to imbibe on duty, but you get what you pay for. Apparently, Petrov wasn't paying enough.

Although Koo figured the time for his disguise was pretty much over this close to the target, it might buy him some time to get closer. He began to walk up the stairs, not making any attempt at stealth, and in fact making an effort to be non-stealthy. After a few steps, the guard took notice.

He dropped the dopestick and picked up an automatic shotgun, primitive but efficient in close quarters. "Hey, you! Get out of here. These floors are off limits."

Koo gave the man his best stupid look and replied, "Hey, okay, okay. My boss told me to come up and fix some stupid drain. No need to get all violent about it."

The young Hawke had meanwhile closed the distance by a few more steps.

The guard gestured with his gun. "Well, I'm saying you can't come up here. Now get!"

Koo figured he'd gotten as close as possible. He raised the palms of his hands as though to show that he wasn't armed. The dart guns attached to his wrists struck the guard in one eye and in the throat. The toxins in the darts attacked the man's central nervous system just about instantaneously, and he dropped to the floor. Koo caught his shotgun before it hit the plascrete and clattered or detonated. The man was already dead.

Koo exited the stairwell on the fiftieth floor and stepped into a hallway. At the far end of the hall was a glassed-in office with the words, Petrov Investments, on the door.

"Ah, a clue!" he said to himself.

Ambling casually toward the office, he noted that there were suspicious bulges and protuberances in the walls, doubtless concealing sensors and weapons, possibly even anti-personnel mines.

"Just a blue collar guy, here to do a job," Koo muttered, thinking unobtrusive thoughts. In Hawke training, mental attitude was a powerful tool. It could aid your itinerant assassin in merging with his surroundings, or even to seemingly disappear. It wasn't magic, exactly, but putting oneself into an energy plane that would be overlooked by most people.

Temujin had scared the shit out of Koo more than once by seemingly stepping out of nowhere, and always when you least expected it. It was as though he really could become invisible. But of course, that was impossible. Wasn't it?

Now, the young Hawke sauntered into the office, and in a confident but somewhat obsequious manner, said to the receptionist, this one clearly of executive quality, "Mister Petrov asked Maintenance to send somebody up. I guess his toilet is backed up or something."

The statuesque blond in the classic, and very expensive, spider-silk catsuit, and who was speaking intently into her desk com, just nodded and waved toward a door to her right. As Koo approached it, there was a click as the latch unlocked.

Koo knew that in any big building like this, something was always broken, and Maintenance was forever running to try to keep up. Nevertheless, there was always some bigshot who was complaining about something and demanding that Maintenance "get a man up here right away and fix this son of a bitch!"

Koo got several levels into the inner office before anybody questioned him again. This time, it was a beefy bodyguard type, so the Hawke knew he was getting close.

"The boss didn't call for anybody, so get out of here, punk!" The man reached to grab Koo by the shoulder and died with a very surprised look on his face.

From this point on, things could get sticky. Moving swiftly but silently, the assassin went through the next door to his left. There were two more no-neck types there, playing cards. With no introduction, Koo launched himself through the air. The edge of his right heel connected with the back of what little neck the thug closest to him had. Their came a crunching crack as his spine separated, and the man went down like a sack of potatoes. His partner started to rise, one hand reaching toward his belt. Koo landed, spun on his planted foot, and crushed this gunman's throat with a side kick.

The gunsel's hand still moved toward his weapon for a moment, but then his body realized it no longer had an air passage. He clutched at his ruined throat and tried to call out. No luck. Koo gave him a grace stroke to the temple. It put him out of the misery of strangling to death and had the fortunate side effect of keeping him from crashing about and making unwanted noise while he tried to breath.

The next office was Petrov's. The money man was on the vidphone when Koo came in. Petrov had his back to the door, facing the holo-image of a man who was wearing an obviously expensive business suit of a cut that Koo immediately identified as being Desotoan. Uniform and clothing recognition was a useful tool in the assassin's toolbox, and it was one of the many skills that Temujin had stressed. Clothing could not only identify the caste or economic level of a potential target, but that same clothing could become one of the guises needed for infiltrating an organization.

The man noticed the movement behind Petrov. He looked irritated and said, "Mister Petrov, I thought this call was to be confidential."

Petrov was startled for a moment, but then he turned to see what his associate was talking about and saw Koo. Or rather, he saw Koo's disguise. All he saw was a maintenance man. "What the hell are you doing in here, punk? Get the hell out!"

Without removing it from his pocket, Koo keyed a tracking device. It would record the source of the call Petrov was on, and very possibly the source.

At the same time, he smiled at the money man. "Why Mister Petrov, I told you I'd be visiting. That was right after you tried to have my family killed on Old Earth."

Petrov's eyes widened in recognition, and he lunged toward a drawer in his desk. He never made it. Koo moved with preternatural swiftness and drove a dagger through the man's hand, pinning him to the desk surface.

There was a yelp from the holo image above the comset, and the display abruptly disappeared.

Koo smiled down at the paymaster. "Gee, Mister Petrov, since you're not going anywhere anytime soon, how about you and I have a nice talk?"

* * * *

Some short time later, Cuchulain Hawke sauntered along the street near Petrov's office building. Apparently, some poor soul had committed suicide by smashing through one of the windows on the fiftieth floor and plummeting to the hard pavement below.

Koo, minus the maintenance man garb, displayed a nominal curiosity in the emergency vehicles clustered in the street below the window.

"They're going to need a sponge," he said softly to himself.

Time to determine his next stop. That guy on the comm had been Desotoan. That meant that things were getting interesting.

## Chapter 13: Atarishii Nihon

While it was true that spacecraft the size of the Celestia, or most warships for that matter, couldn't ordinarily land dirtside, private yachts like Gwendolyn had been doing so for quite some time. Money talks, after all. The ability of their ship to land on the planetary surface would be a factor in how the Hawkes decided to carry out any operations on Atarishii Nihon. But much could be accomplished from orbit, including electronic surveillance and system queries.

Of course, Gwendolyn was not strictly a privately owned spacecraft, at least not by an individual. She was registered on Starcastle to Galactica Security, and as the head of the Special Projects Section, Roland Hawke had every right to use her to get around. All on company business, of course. And this investigation was indeed company business, despite the fact that he was accompanied by his brother, Jason. For one thing, they had matching goals and complementary skill sets. They each knew the capabilities of the other, and they knew that they could trust the other to cover their back.

This could be invaluable in tight situations. In fact, Roland had tried to bring Jason on board with Galactica shortly after the Bishti business, but Jason wasn't interested. He'd only gotten involved in that mess because he'd had a personal stake; Kristin. Once done with the danger to the woman he loved, the older Hawke brother would have been perfectly happy to retire to a life of peace and politics. At least that's what he'd said. Roland had a sneaking suspicion that that peaceful life may have begun to pall. After all, their father had raised them to be doers, not the sort that could sit around for long. Roland also had enough sense to not press the issue though.

Jason said, "So I take it you're figuring on tracing these geeks through the tickets that they bought to get from here to Earth?"

Roland sat at his ease on an acceleration seat now configured into a couch. "That would be correct."

Jason looked around and said, "So who's going to do that little chore? I mean, I wouldn't want you to put yourself out or anything."

Roland covered his mouth in a fake yawn. "Actually, Gwendolyn is tracing the ticket sale even as we speak." He chuckled. "You really should learn to let technology do the job whenever possible, big brother."

Jason waved him off. "Yeah, yeah, yeah! I just want to get moving on this mission. I'm afraid that any chickens here are going to fly the coop before we can find them. After all, they bought the ticket a couple of weeks ago now."

Roland nodded.

"I want to find them too. Worst case, we may have to track them to their next destination. But I guarantee we will find them." He gave Jason a grim smile. "In case I hadn't mentioned it, they pissed me off a bit too." His normally bland, slightly superior expression turned grim for a moment. Jason had seen sharks that looked friendlier. "No one tries to kill the Moderator on my watch. Two of those dead Bodyguards were friends of mine."

Then, he smiled again, and it was as if that other Roland had never existed. But Jason remembered, and he knew that his brother was looking forward to getting some of his own payback on the Hashishiyun, and whoever might want to help them out.

Scott Douglas, Roland's mercenary pilot of choice, came over the intercom. "Mister Hawke, Gwendolyn has a fix for you."

A soft female voice came onto the ship's sound system. "The ticket used by the assassins was bought from a travel agency for three two-way tickets on Trans-System Spacelines. The transaction was handled by a travel agency, Samurai Travel, LLC, here in Osaka. I have traced the financial trail, and the funds came from the Bishti Consulate."

Jason gave a wolf's grin. Unconsciously, his expression closely mirrored the one he'd seen on his brother minutes before. He said, "Ah, our old friends! I would have thought that our forcible retirement of their previous management might have persuaded them to change direction. Guess not. Once a scumbag, always a scumbag." He looked at Roland. "Think we should pay them a visit?"

Roland sounded a hard laugh. "I think it's a moral imperative. After all, we need to remind them what happens when you screw around with the Hawke family! They seem to have forgotten."

* * * *

In spite of sophisticated sensor suites and the implications of modern technology, night remained the best time to execute a covert infiltration of potential enemy-held territory. And in spite of the fact that Nihon was an ally of the Confederation, the Bishti Consulate could certainly be considered enemy territory, especially if, as seemed likely, they were aiding and abetting the Hashishiyun.

Thus it was that two ghostly figures floated through the Nihonese atmosphere on heavily-stealthed gravsleds, spiraling in from Gwendolyn's low planetary orbit toward the capital city of Osaka and the building that housed the Bishti Consulate. The night intruders could have used guidable parachutes, but even low orbit was too high for a HALO jump. Besides, the gravsleds were more controllable, and they would be coming in over a major city. Landing on the wrong building would be embarrassing at best, and lethal at worst.

In a firefight like they'd engaged in on Bishti, and each of the other combat experiences the brothers had endured, survival was all too frequently a binary set. You either lived or died. Any wounds tended to be fatal or something that could be lived with to carry on the mission. They'd come out of that other mess because of training, experience, and luck. But you couldn't always depend on luck. A guard could come outside for a dopestick or a slug of his favorite mood-altering drink, just as the supposedly covert team was starting its infiltration. More than one operation had been blown that way. So the Hawkes did everything they could to insure that the surprises would be on their side, and not the other way around. This was a drop onto a hot LZ, and they were going in armed for big game.

As it happened, there were two guards on the roof of the consulate. The Bishtians could learn from experience after all, Jason thought. Without needing to communicate verbally, Jason took the guard on the right, and Roland took the guard on the left. They used silenced carbines for the job, and both guards dropped just moments before the two assailants touched down on their sleds.

They had discussed armament before the mission. Carbines made sense, since the action would be urban and mostly indoors. Each brother also carried a silenced handgun, a combat knife, and a short sword. Both wore light battle armor. Although the sights on the carbines had a sensor suite that included infrared and motion radar, neither of the Hawkes used night vision goggles. There were multiple reasons for this. First and foremost, they'd been raised to rely on their natural senses, which their father had made sure were trained to an advanced degree. In most cases, their night vision was as good as most soldiers would have been using goggles. This had the added advantage that eyes could adjust more quickly to changing light sources, whereas night vision goggles could be overloaded with sudden bursts of luminescence, like, say flash grenades. Also, no Hawke wanted to sacrifice their excellent peripheral vision, which all goggles did to some extent. True, there were night vision contact lenses, but even those had drawbacks, similar to those of goggles.

One thing that the two trained assassins did wear, however, was military-grade chamos. The picotech smart material of the combat utility uniforms rendered them virtually invisible, since it reflected the background almost perfectly. Nothing was absolutely perfect, of course, and an alert observer could still see a blur as the chamo-wearer moved, but that was frequently too late. Standing still, the itinerant assassin or spec warfare operative was the next best thing to invisible.

The sleds touched down, and the two dismounted quickly. They checked the bodies, but both guards were safely dead. Double-tap head shots can have that effect.

Roland and Jason moved quickly to the only door down into the three-story building. Some of the other embassies and consulates had much larger high-rise abodes, but Bishti was smaller and poorer. As they ghosted down the hallway, it was obvious that the caretakers were slovenly at best. Jason had seen many planets like Bishti, and their work ethic was considerably different than most worlds in the Confederation. No one had a good explanation for that, but he'd seen it was true, and the condition of this building exemplified that.

The moved silently down the hall of the third story. Temujin had always stressed clearing a building from the top down. That way, you left no enemies behind you. This floor was mostly residential. It seemed to be given over to lower functionaries, none of whom were out and about. Several of the rooms reeked of dopestick. They took the stairs down to the second floor. Using a microsnoop to peer down the hall before opening the door fully, they could see two guards standing before some ornate double doors. The two brothers exchanged glances, and Roland drew his right hand across his throat in a throat-cutting gesture. Jason would have made the same call if he'd been alone.

They cracked the door open just enough to poke the barrels of their carbines out. The silenced weapons coughed, and the tracking heads guided the slugs into the brains of the two guards, both of whom dropped silently to the floor. One guard spasmed for a few seconds, kicking one heel against the wall, but then he was still.

Jason and Roland remained in position to see if taking out the guards would generate a reaction. After thirty long seconds, no one came running, so they ghosted out into the carpeted hallway.

They got to the double-doored chamber that the guards had been standing in front of. Jason took the right side of the doors, while Roland took the left side. With a nod, Jason knelt down and tried the door latch. It was unlocked. Very carefully, a millimeter at a time, he eased it open. When there was a crack about two inches wide, he peeked around the edge.

A plasma blast blew a large chunk out of the edge of the door about a foot above his head. Jason pulled back, and both brothers hit the floor as several more blasts perforated the doors. They stopped finally, and the Hawkes stood and kicked in both doors simultaneously. They entered what appeared to be a large conference room. A Bishti fedayeen was just reloading his plasma rifle, and two others were looking on, assault weapons in their hands. Apparently, the idea that the plasma blasts would not kill anyone on the other side of the doors hadn't occurred to them. Now, with the two Hawkes barely visible in their chamos smashing into the room, they tried to bring their weapons to bear. Both onlookers died before they could get off a shot. Jason flew across the room and kicked the barrel of the plasma weapon upward. He followed that with a kick to the fedayeen's family jewels. A very hard kick. The man collapsed into a moaning fetal position.

Doors to either side of the room slammed open and three of the green-clad Hashishiyun rushed in.

Jason had thoroughly briefed Roland on the attack on the Moderator on Starcastle, and both knew that the body and heads of the Alamut assassins were armored internally.

Roland already had his carbine to his shoulder, so he triggered a burst of high-velocity slugs at the man rushing in his direction. Two bullets hit the man in the forehead, rocking his head back but not killing him. The third slug entered his right eye, and he collapsed.

Two more Greenies rushed the dimly seen Jason. He got off one shot that slammed one of the Hashishiyun back, but didn't kill him. The other assassin closed quickly. Jason grabbed one of the outstretched arms that the killer was trying to grapple with, sat down, and put a foot in the man's stomach. The Hashishiyun flew in a flat trajectory, directly into a wall, becoming embedded up to his shoulders.

Jason immediately faced the other attacker who had recovered his momentum to attack in his turn. In a classic iaijutsu move, Jason drew his wakizashi and stepped across the man's path. With the razor sharp blade and the man's own forward momentum, the killer's head parted company with his body and bounced in the opposite direction from his rushing body.

As the final attacker pulled himself out of the wall and turned to kill the intruders, Roland put his pistol under the man's chin and pulled the trigger several times. The outside of the man's skull really was armored, because none of the bullets blew out the back of his head. Apparently, they ricocheted around inside, however, because his brains blew out through his eyes.

When there was no more immediate threat, Jason took his bloody blade and wiped it on the shirt of the fedayeen who was just beginning to come out of his jellied-testicle-induced curl and was trying to reach for his weapon. At the touch of the bloody blade, the man froze.

Roland came over and asked, "Are there any more of these assholes?"

The man started to shake his head, but Jason's blade was at his throat. He responded with a shaky, "no. These were all of the green ones."

Roland went on, "And why were they here on Nihon?"

The man didn't answer, but Jason's blade pushed a bit, and a trickle of blood ran down the man's throat. "No! I do not know their whole mission! But it is on the console in the other room. Please! That is all I know!"

Roland looked at Jason and nodded. With a quick, sideways movement, the short sword slashed across the fedayeen's throat, and he convulsed as his windpipe and both carotid arteries were slashed open. A bubbling sound was quickly quenched in the rush of blood as the man died.

Once again, Jason used the man's shirt to clean his blade, which he now sheathed.

Roland went directly to the adjoining office. The desk console was turned on, and when Roland slapped a pocket AI onto the side of it, it began to disgorge everything it knew. The information was transmitted directly to Gwendolyn's data banks. One thing caught Roland's attention, however.

"Ah, just as I suspected. The Hashishiyun were here to kill off the highest officers in the Nihonese government." He looked at his brother. "I'll have Gwendolyn send their police the information just before we leave. I don't feel like wasting time dealing with them right now."

Jason nodded. "Agreed. Are there any clues as to other cells?"

Roland paged through some displays. Then he nodded. "Oh yeah. They've apparently got something going on Achaea."

"Cool. We go to Achaea next then."

Roland looked thoughtful. "Say, didn't Richard say something about him and Kat going to Achaea?"

Jason said, "Oh-oh."

# Chapter 14: Rebels

Richard Hawke was slumming. That is, he was walking through the slums. He wore his usual black robe, not unusual in this environment, and that allowed him to blend in to his surroundings. While not actually invisible, he wasn't particularly noticeable, either. He also made a point of not projecting his personal energies onto the world around him. It was frequently surprising how that would allow him, or any of the Hawkes, to just float through an area, while the locals went about their business, blissfully disregarding him.

Kat was over at the Confederation Space Facility. She'd been asked to aid in setting up the plans for confronting the incoming Desotoan flotilla. As it happened, she had the most recent actual combat experience. Yet, Kat did not try to overwhelm the local commanders with her awesomeness. She made it clear that they were in charge, and she was just there to help out in any way she could.

In one corner of his mind, Richard hoped that was all that it would come to. He had no particular desire to see her go into space combat again.

Having said that, she was busy, and Richard had decided to occupy himself with seeking out the leaders of the rebellion. He had somehow neglected to mention his investigation to Kat before he'd left. She was pretty busy with other things, anyway.

Richard didn't like the smell of this "rebellion." It was too convenient, and the Desotoan "intervention" was too pat. He was pretty sure there was some relationship between the two. With any kind of luck, he could get a whiff of what that relationship was. The Desotoans had used the tactic of planting agents in other societies on planets that they wanted to acquire before this, and it seemed likely that such was going on here too.

Several of the rebel attacks had been on local police officers in this part of the town, so this seemed like as good a place to start as any. After all, the local cops were mostly occupied with the ritzier sections. That was good. Those places needed to be inspected and protected as well. But the former Zen monk figured that you could hide a lot of sins in this sort of run-down district, with all its warehouses and abandoned buildings.

Then, he heard weapons being discharged somewhere ahead of him. He did not hear the sizzle-crash of plasma weapons, but rather the hard crack of projectile weapons. He'd been trained to distinguish the different kind of weapons not only visually, but also by sound. There was at least one high powered rifle being used, possibly two. There was also the string-of-firecrackers sound of machine pistols, along with the smaller crack of sidearms. This was probably just the sort of action he'd been looking for.

Richard eased up to the corner of the building on the end of the street he'd been walking on. A quick peek around the corner showed him a Mycenaean ground effect police vehicle that had crashed into a storefront. He could see uniformed police officers using the vehicle as cover from a building across the street from them. As Richard watched, he saw a flash from the roof of that building, and a window in the police cruiser smashed to pieces. One of the officers cried out, wounded by either the bullet or shrapnel from the window. Richard took a moment to consider the implications of that.

Police vehicles had glass that would withstand anything a civilian firearm could hit them with. Ergo, the sniper, or more likely snipers, on the roof was using a military-grade slug weapon. The bad guys had the range on the cops, who apparently only had small arms. They were trapped.

Without revealing himself too much, Richard studied the building occupied by the rebel ambush team.

It was five stories tall, made of local brick, with no obvious protuberances. It was basically a brick box with no windows on the ground floor. That was probably both for environmental and security purposes. The rebels would most likely have booby-trapped the stairs and lifts. That would be a basic safety precaution.

No matter. He was a Hawke.

Richard made his way quickly around the adjoining buildings, keeping to cover and concealment as much of the way as possible. No one appeared to notice him, and soon he was standing at the base of one of the side walls that had no doors. The rebels would most likely have seen no need to guard a wall with no ingress.

The erstwhile monk drew in a deep breath, finding his center almost immediately. Then, he began to climb up the side of the wall. Moving his arms and legs in a manner similar to a lizard on a garden wall, Richard moved up the wall. One floor, then two floors. He concentrated on focusing his Ki inwards toward the bricks, with a bit of upward focus as well. This was an ancient technique handed down through the Hawke family. Temujin Hawke had been able to move up and down sheer walls and cliffs as quickly as most men could walk down a sidewalk, and he trained his sons in that technique. In no sense did Richard consider himself the equal of his father, but what he was doing right now would seem impossible to most anyone else.

No one gave an alarm. Apparently, no one was looking in this direction. Richard reached the lip of the roof and peered over the edge, showing only the very top of his head down to his eyes.

To his right, on the side that the cops faced, he saw two men hunched over near the low parapet. The loud crack of a "smokepole" projectile weapon sounded. They were still engaging the police patrol. To his left there were two more men in a similar position. He'd been right. They were covering the other entrance. And straight across from him was one last man. He was totally focused on the door in a small structure that had apparently let them onto the roof. Presumably, the structure held internal stairs and possibly the machinery for the building's lift mechanism.

Richard oozed over the parapet and stood. Anyone watching him would have seen him apparently walk casually across the roof. A watcher might have wondered if he weren't some sort of hologram, though, for he made no sound. Legends surrounded the Hawkes, crediting them with powers of invisibility, flying, and even teleportation. They were none of those things, but more.

The man facing the door to the roof died never knowing anyone else was around. Richard glided toward the two facing the rear entrance. The man with the rifle dropped without a sound, but his partner caught a flicker of movement and began to turn. A cry died on his lips as his neck and larynx were crushed.

Richard turned and moved swiftly toward the other two. The spotter turned and shouted. It was the last sound he ever made.

* * * *

On the street below, one of the officers who had been pinned down by the snipers cocked his head. He said, "What was that?"

His partner, badly wounded and crouched in the cover of their perforated vehicle, replied testily, "What was what?"

His partner was scanning the roofs above them, very carefully, so as to not provide and easy target. Their patrol sergeant had made that mistake, and his brains were leaking into the gutters.

The man's eyes widened. "Holy shit!"

"What?" The wounded cop looked up to see a body, and then another come flying out from the edge of the roof above them. One emitted a ululating cry as he descended. Then it hit, and was thereafter silent.

Then there was a huge BANG from the top of the building. Both officers ducked, but nothing happened. It would be some time before they took the initiative to leave cover and enter the building.

* * * *

With all targets serviced, Richard picked up the dead rebel's body and through it down the steps, quickly stepping back. There was a large explosion from the stairwell. He'd been right. The rebels had boobytrapped the path to the roof.

No matter. He slipped over the opposite wall and made his way to the alley below.

"Work, work, work," he muttered quietly. There were bound to be other rebel cells in this part of the city. Richard Hawke would find them, and after a while, they would be no more.

# Chapter 15: Engagement

Kat Dunvegan was in the main situation room of the Confederation fighter base plotting various attack profiles with the group's tac officers when the holocomm at the end of the room activated. There appeared the head and shoulders of a man with what she considered idiotic amounts of gold braid on his hat and uniform. The breast of his uniform blouse was all but invisible beneath a breastplate of colorful medals. Given that Achaea hadn't been to war with anyone in over a decade, Kat momentarily wondered what they were all for. Surely they couldn't all be good conduct awards!

As soon as the comm link was established, the man spoke.

"I am High Admiral Lysandros Maimonides, Commander of all Achaean Space Forces!" Kat could hear the capital letters the admiral put into his title. He went on, "because I am the highest ranking officer in this system, I am taking command of the Achaean fleet and of the Confederation military spacecraft stationed here as well!"

Blaustein stepped forward. "High Admiral, I am Colonel Gareth Blaustein. Our craft are fully armed and fueled. What can our two fighter squadrons do to help you against the incoming Desotoan fleet?"

Maimonides looked at Blaustein with some disdain. "My task force consists of one heavy cruiser and two destroyers. Your squadrons will fly close escort on my force, acting to intercept any incoming missiles or vessels. My ships will do the real work of stopping the Desotoan scum!"

Blaustein nodded. "Of course, we will act as escorts, Sir. But might I suggest that we detail one of the squadrons to harass the enemy ships? Fighters can be effective against destroyers, at least, Sir."

The High Admiral became very red in the face. "You fighter types are always too cocky! You will fly close escort, as I ordered! Your squadrons will lift immediately, or I'll see you hanged for treason!"

The comm shut down. Kat walked over to Gareth and said in a dry tone, "so much for the voice of reason."

The Marine commander shook his head. "The man is an idiot. He has no clue how to fight a modern war, and his orders will get us all killed while accomplishing nothing!"

Kat nodded. "From what I hear, his cruiser is a candidate for a museum, and his two destroyers are two-thirds the size of modern craft."

He looked around the control room.

"Actually, I don't think any museum would take that piece of junk he calls a cruiser. Oh, it looks pretty, but its systems are over ten years old, and the missiles haven't been serviced by anyone who knew what he was doing in quite some time. On the other hand, he's right about being the senior Confederation officer in this system, damn it!" In a much louder voice, he called, "Okay, boys and girls, you heard the man. Saddle up!"

Kat said, "I feel sorry for you and your guys. I know what it's like to go up against a superior force."

He gave her a long look. "Yes, you do, don't you? And you have way more recent combat experience than anyone in my squadron. How would you feel about flying with us as a supernumerary? I can't guarantee you'll get paid, or even that you'll survive the experience, but I have a fighter that just came fresh out of maintenance, and I'm short a pilot."

She grinned. "Boy, you sure know how to sweet-talk a girl! Okay, I'm in."

He grinned back. "Okay, get suited up, Lieutenant. We've got places to go and people to blow up!"

* * * *

The Confederation Viper space fighters took off and headed off-planet on impulse engines. Kat was on Blaustein's right wing, although the stubby protuberances called wings on space fighters were more hard points on which to hang ordinance than real, functional wings. The craft had positional impulsers and anti-gravity to control their maneuvers and ascent/descents. Plus, the whole craft was built on the lifting body concept. Even dead stick, the Vipers had something of a glide path, albeit a very steep glide path. On the other hand, the fighters were not hyperspace-capable. The only power plants that they had were impulse drives, albeit very large impulse drives for such a small hull.

They rendezvoused with the outbound Achaean ships as ordered, about a third of the way to the edge of the Achaean system. Even from the distance they kept between them, she could see that the Achaean craft were somewhat the worse for wear. Not surprising, considering their age. As far as she'd been able to tell, and from what she'd heard, the Achaean spacemen were top notch, though. They were going to need to be.

The Confederation fighters broke into four elements: high cover, low cover, cover to the front, and cover to the rear. The four elements were designated Turban One (Front), Turban Two (Port), Turban Three (Starboard), and Turban Four (Top). Sensor readings had been updated constantly ever since the Desotoan bogies had entered the system. It appeared that they had no fighters of their own, nor would they need them, in all likelihood. Conventional wisdom said that fighter spacecraft couldn't take out a military warship, and the Desotoans outnumbered the

Achaeans two to one. Even that was deceptive, for the Dons' ships were considerably newer and presumably more effective technologically. Blaustein was right. All things being equal, the Achaeans were toast, and their idiot admiral was well on the way to taking the Confederation fighters along with them.

As was standard procedure for most Terran-derived space navies, the Achaean fleet considered "up" and "down" as relative to the north and south poles of the main planet as it stood in relation to the solar system's ecliptic. Humans in general, and fighting forces in particular, needed references to coordinate their movements, and although such directions didn't absolutely exist in space, relationship to a system's ecliptic provided a three-dimensional topography that could be used for such reference.

So Kat was flying top cover with Turban Four on Colonel Blaustein's wing when they got the call from the flights stationed out in front of the Achaeans.

"Vampire, vampire, vampire! Multiple missile signatures heading our way. Estimate over one hundred drives inbound!"

Blaustein was cool and calm, although Kat thought she detected a slight edge in his voice as he said, "Okay, boys and girls. Here's the part where we earn our princely salaries."

There were multiple-source chuckles across the net, but nobody else spoke.

"Go to full active sensors. Link your firing AIs and choose your targets. We don't want to waste our counter-missiles by firing at the same target." He paused. "Wait for it. Wait for it. "Now! Fire as you bear!"

About one hundred ship-killing missiles were accelerating toward the Achaean task force. Kat figured it could hardly be called a fleet, although Admiral Maimonides certainly considered it one. She fleetingly wondered why the Achaeans hadn't launched as well, but then realized that their older technology missiles probably didn't have the range. Surprisingly, Maimonides was doing something intelligent in holding his fire until he had a real target solution.

The counter-missiles began impacting on the incoming vampires and energy blossoms began to appear on her screen as the big ship-killers exploded while still thousands of miles away. Maybe the Achaean admiral wasn't so stupid after all. The Desotoans were essentially wasting ammo, launching at extreme range and depending on their newer-style weapons to overwhelm the little Achaean force. As long as the Confed fighters had counter missiles, the Desotoan salvoes just weren't going to get through at maximum range.

But now the ship-killers were getting close, and the fighters' supply of counter-missiles was getting low.

Blaustein called, "Front CAP, break right. Get out of the way and let the heavies do their thing."

The fighter element in front of the Achaean task force broke out to their right and gave the Achaean warships a clear field of fire. Heavier counter-missiles from the destroyers lashed out, and more and more of the incoming missiles ceased to exist.

But there were a hundred incoming missiles. Inevitably, some got through both the counter-missiles and the close-in batteries. Kat saw a flash off to her port as one of the destroyers took a hit. The vessel kept coming on, so it must not have been fatal. Several missiles detonated just short of the Achaean cruiser. She knew that some debris had to have impacted the larger vessel, but say what you like about Maimonides, he didn't flinch in the face of enemy fire.

Then the range had closed, the wave of ship-killers had been dealt with, and the Achaean ships fired their own ship-killing missiles.

Kat figured that now the shit was about to really hit the fan.

# Chapter 16: Counterpunch

As the man with the scimitar upraised rushed at him screaming, Richard Hawke watched and waited. Even as the blade began to come down to split him in two, the Hawke moved in under the blade, grabbed the man's shirt front, and sat down, lifting one foot into the man's stomach. Pulling with his hands and thrusting upwards with his foot, he propelled the swordsman over his shoulders. As it happened, the cornice at the edge of the roof was very close to Richard's head. Therefore, instead of the throw depositing the killer flat on his back as generally happened in practice, the man was sent soaring into space. As it turned out, he could not fly.

Richard stood up and looked around. Once again, he had counter-ambushed a group of snipers that had pinned down an Achaean police patrol. He had reasoned with the sniper team in the time-honored Hawke way, and now they all lay silent, except for the scream that dopplered away from him, only to end abruptly.

Richard eeled over the cornice and down the wall on the side away from the police and continued on his one-man mission.

* * * *

"We are being attacked by commandoes!" the voice wailed from the communicator.

The Hamadi holy warrior looked at the voice-only comm he held in disbelief. Putting it back to his ear, he replied, "Commandoes? There are no Achaean commandoes! What uniforms did these men wear?"

"They wore black robes!" said the local rebel leader. "They have already killed at least three of our sniper teams! They are like ghosts!"

"Ghosts?"

"And they can fly! They have attacked us from over the side of buildings where there are no lifts and no stairs. They must be able to fly."

"Ghosts who can fly," the Hamadian commander repeated in a flat voice.

"Yes! Yes! They are ghosts who can fly!"

"Enough! You attempt to cover your cowardice with unbelievable stories of imaginary ghost commandoes!"

"But…"

"Enough, I said! I will take care of this myself."

The commander broke down the comm and turned to the other men in the room. “Ahmad, take a squad toward the location of these so-called commando attacks. Kill any police, soldiers, or commandoes you encounter.”

Ahmad bowed and replied, “as you wish, Commander.”

With a head gesture, he gathered the five men of his elite squad and headed out the door.

Commander Ibrahim Mohammed turned to the other men in the room, three lean men dressed all in green. “We will follow a bit behind Ahmad and his men. If there are indeed any commandoes out there, you will kill them. Kill them all!”

Without speaking, the Hashishiyun nodded. So it would be.

* * * *

Finding the first three sniper teams had been easy. Now, they seemed to be becoming more wary. In one way, that was to the good, as far as Richard was concerned. If they were more wary, then fewer Achaean officials would die. On the other hand, it made the rebels harder to find.

Nevertheless, the erstwhile monk wanted to see if there was anything else he could do before he called it a day. The combat had been stimulating, although with his skills, the bad guys hadn’t really had much of a chance. They just hadn’t known that until it was much too late.

Richard spotted the team of Hamadi commandos before they spotted him, and he faded into a shadowed doorway. These gunmen were moving much better than the sniper teams he'd taken out. They were deployed more like a combat team in hostile territory, which made sense. The sniper teams had been fairly lax, assuming they were safe on top of the roofs, and that had made Richard's job easier, at least for a Hawke.

Of course, Richard appearing as if by magic (to the snipers anyway) over the side of the buildings had surprised the rebel snipers, and surprise could be a powerful force. Hmmm. How to surprise the Hamadis?

The six-man Hamadi commando team moved slowly, checking and clearing any alcoves, alleys, or other potential hiding places. The reports had mentioned multiple commandos. Although the team commander, Captain of the Faithful Ahmad Jaffari, was skeptical of the reports from the local rebels, he felt that he would be foolish to ignore them completely. Somebody had taken down those sniper teams, whether it was the reported "commandoes in black robes" or not. Jaffari had been trained by the Hamadi army, and, although he had never tasted combat, he had no qualms about killing the enemies of his home planet. That was especially true after all the destruction that had been visited upon Hamad by the Confederation agents just a few years since.

The Confederation had denied sending agents to his planet, but Ahmad had seen the reports that over a hundred elite troops had been dropped onto Hamad, killing the ruler, his main general, and destroying their spaceport.

Later news stories from the Confederation had claimed that all that destruction had been accomplished by four brothers. What nonsense! That story was only suited for the Confed media, where the credible infidels would believe just about anything, as long as it reinforced their illusion of arrogant self-reliance.

Ahmad's squad was moving slowly down a side street, with two fire teams of three men each. That way, they could cover each other, no matter what quarter they were attacked from. Ahmad himself was second back from his point man, who had the position of maximum danger. If anything or anyone took out the point, Ahmad would be able to deploy his men's fire onto the source of the threat.

There was a slight sound directly behind him, and the squad leader glanced in that direction. Oddly, there was nobody behind him. He looked back at the other fire team that should have been trailing them. They weren't there either. Alarm bells began ringing in the Hamadi's head. He pivoted back toward his front, but his point man had disappeared as well. Quickly, the commando leader put his back to the wall of the building he stood next to, his slug rifle covering the area around him. What had happened to his men?

The loop of razor-thin wire dropped around his neck, and before he could react, it tightened. The monomolecular cord cut through his throat and carotid arteries. The last thing that Ahmad saw was his own arterial blood gushing out in front of him.

* * * *

As Ahmad dropped, Commander Mohammed gave his command to the Hashishiyun, “There they are! Go! Kill the Achaean assassins!”

The three men in green moved with blinding speed in the direction of the Hamadi squad leaders dead body.

It was time to kill.

# Chapter 17: Spacekat

The capital ships of the two space forces had closed to energy weapons' range, and it was time for the fighters to get out of the way. That was the opinion and the orders of the Achaean Admiral Maimonides, anyway.

Colonel Blaustein agreed, but he had his own agenda. "All Turban elements, break to port! Form on me."

The Vipers flashed off to the left of the Achaean formations as the heavies engaged. High-power energy beams flashed across the darkness of space, momentarily outshining the stars. Metal was smashed and torn, and men died.

As the squadron regrouped, Blaustein called, "Okay, Turbans, now we really get to work. I'm guessing everybody's pretty low on counter-missiles, so we going to do this fast and get the hell out.

"Turban One, you're first, hit the destroyers hard. Turban Two, Three, and Four, you'll follow. Go for their thrusters, gun mounts, and command centers. Don't waste around, and don't go for a second pass. Hit 'em hard and bug out. We'll be right behind you." He paused. "Let's show these bastards who the big dog really is in this sector. Execute!"

The Confederation's Vipers were offensively armed with plasma cannon and missiles. No one expected the missiles to be of much use in this engagement, since they were designed primarily to take out other fighters. The 50 mm plasma cannon, on the other hand, could certainly do some damage. And it was time to show the Desotoans just how much damage a Viper could cause.

The fighters of Turban One peeled off and blasted toward the destroyers on the enemy's starboard. The destroyers were apparently concentrating totally on the big Achaean warships, because they didn't fire on the Vipers as they came arrowing in. The four fighters opened up with their plasma cannon, and explosions walked across the surface of the two closest destroyers. The Desotoan shields stopped some of the bolts, but they apparently had full power to their shields facing the Achaean formation, because an awful lot of the plasma bolts got through. Kat could see explosions walking across the hulls of the two warships in the wake of the bolts. And then Turban One was past, and it was the turn of Turban Two.

The Desotoans were ready for them this time, and both missiles and energy beams flashed across space towards the fighters. One of the Vipers exploded in a flash of plasma, but it was closely followed by one of the destroyers, which also exploded, flinging the remaining Turban Two fighters across space on the blast front.

"Okay, Three and Four, "said Blaustein, "we're going after the two destroyers on the far side of the formation. I'll go in first. Follow my lead, and fire at whatever targets present themselves."

The eight Vipers went up and over the enemy formation, keeping out of firing range and accelerating as fast as possible to make the bad guys' firing solutions as difficult as possible.

"Here we go!" the Confed squadron commander called out. Then he peeled off and dived down towards the outermost destroyer of the Desotoan formation.

Kat thought that if they could bleed the Desotoans enough, they might call it quits. Hey, it could happen. And given the disparity of forces, that hope was about all they had.

Then it was Kat's turn. As her fighter screamed down toward the Desotoans, the outboard destroyer exploded in a massive fireball. The colonel must have hit something big, possibly a fusion bottle.

Then Kat's fighter was caught in the grip of the

blast wave and hurled across the rear of the enemy formation. The Viper tumbled end over end, centrifugal force slapping her from side to side in the narrow cockpit.

Finally, she regained control, and checked her instruments. Some minor damage to the hull plates, but all systems were still green. But she'd lost all track of the destroyer she'd been targeting. It was then that she realized there was something in front of her though. Something big.

Kat realized she was on a screaming ballistic course towards the stern of one of the Desotoan cruisers. Energy bolts began flashing by her fighter. She thought she must have surprised them. They had known that no Achaean ships were behind them, and it probably never occurred to them that a fighter would make a lone run on a ship of the line. After all, that would be insane. But that was what was happening.

"Oh shit," she said to herself, "Spacekat is in hot!"

With that, she cut loose with everything she had at the stern impellers, which were glowing with blue energy. All her anti-fighter missiles, her anti-ship missiles, her remaining counter-missiles, and her bow cannon blasted outward at the enemy cruiser.

The enemy energy bolts were getting close now. And then space flared white and red around her, she heard metal screaming, and for Kat, the universe went black.

## Chapter 18: Asp Strike

Lieutenant Commander James Lewis spoke to the commanders of his ASP boats. “Men, as you have most likely heard by now, there is a major engagement of the Achaean forces and an incoming Desotoan task force. The Achaeans are badly outnumbered and outgunned.”

CPO Wilson asked, “how come the Achaean admiral didn’t have us ship out with them?”

Lewis shook his head. “I don’t know for sure, but I think he actually forgot about us. From what I’ve heard, he’s a classic big-ship admiral, and he probably just wrote us off as useless.”

Wilson gave his commander a shrewd look. “I guess that would mean that he did not give us direct orders to not engage either then, wouldn’t it sir?”

Commander Lewis laughed.

"Ah, the Navy way. Anything that is not specifically forbidden is legal. As it happens, Chief, in this particular instance, I agree with you." He looked around at the commanding officers of his squadron and gave them a feral grin. "Get moving people. We're going hunting!"

Chief Wilson had seen to it that all the ASP boats were fully fueled and fully armed. The ASP crews had been through tons of simulations, but the ASPs had never been tested in real combat. One way or another, that was about to change.

ASP 100 was Lewis' personal command, although he was also in command of the entire squadron of ten boats. Because it was a command vessel, ASP 100, called "Hun" by her crew, had more capable communications and one less ship-killing torpedo than the other boats in the squadron.

The ASP squadron commander had delegated lifting off and initial course setting to Chief Wilson, while he studied the sensors and tried to get a comprehensive picture of how the engagement was shaping up. The two forces had indeed engaged, and it looked like at least two of the enemy destroyers were out of the fight. At this range, it was hard to get all the details, but in general, the Achaeans were giving a surprisingly good account of themselves, probably due to the Confed fighters' help. But the odds were still stacked against the local forces, and they were going to need some help.

Having said that, Commander Lewis had no intention of going head to head with cruisers or destroyers unless he had absolutely no alternative. The ASPs were designed to take on much smaller and more lightly armed spacecraft, but Lewis and his officers had been wargaming how to successfully engage real ships of the line, and, based on that, he'd come up with a plan.

Lewis called up the squadron comm and said, "Okay, folks, the good guys are in a bad situation, and we're going to try to help them out. I have no intention of sacrificing any of our boats to no purpose, however. When I sign off, I want all boats to go to full EMCON; no comms, no active emissions. I want us to be a hole in space as far as the Desotoans are concerned. We're going to dive below the ecliptic, and come up beneath the enemy task force, and I want to hit them hard and fast, and then get out." He paused. "Now, let's get to it. The course is laid into all your ship AIs." Lewis flashed a grin a hunting tiger would have been proud of. "Let's go kill some bad guys!"

* * * *

Once they reached cruising speed, the ASPs cut power and proceeded ballistically. Per Lewis' orders, they also maintained strict emissions control. No comms, and no active sensor sweeps. The good news was that the part of the system that they were heading for was bright with flares of energies. The blasts of missiles and torpedoes, the flare of plasma cannon, and the occasional eruption of exploding gases were easily discernible even on passive sensors.

Lewis knew that those sterile phenomena on his displays actually meant that men and machines were being rent asunder in the darkness of space. People were dying, some horribly. But he steeled himself to his job, and his training helped keep him focused.

The Desotoan fleet was still decelerating, while the Achaeans were still accelerating. This resulted in a passing engagement, but it seemed to go on forever.

With all the competing trajectories and maneuvering, a human being would have been hard put to calculate a coherent closing maneuver, but that was what artificial intelligences were for. Lewis punched in what he wanted the boats to do, and the AI figured the appropriate speeds, accelerations, and trajectories to accomplish that goal.

Using IFF codes and drive signatures, the AI analyzed which ships were Desotoan and which were Achaean. These were careted appropriately on Lewis' tactical display. The ASP Commander used this data to formulate an attack scenario. He saved it and sent a data burst to the ASP squadron.

Moments later, still maintaining tight EMCON, the boats broke into two elements. Lewis figured that the enemy cruisers were the more important targets, so each ASP element homed in on one of the Desotoan heavies.

As the torpedo boats came screaming up from beneath the Desotoans, one of the cruisers suddenly disintegrated before them. Several huge explosions in the stern drive area were followed by a series of internal detonations that walked through the hull, culminating in a huge flare that had to be at least one fusion bottle going. The huge spacecraft broke in half, each huge piece cartwheeling away from the blast epicenter, along with some fairly large other fragments which the ASPs had to dodge. Some of those smaller fragments were as large as a whole torpedo boat.

For a split second before the initial explosions, Lewis had thought that he'd seen a fighter icon closing on the stern of the cruiser. A kamikaze perhaps? The Confed space fighter jocks certainly weren't trained in that direction, but combat could do funny things to a man's point of view.

Speaking of which, "All ships, focus on the remaining cruiser. Let's take this bastard out!"

The swarm of ASP boats closed on the remaining Desotoan heavy warship, which was already streaming air and debris. There was blood in the water, and the sharks were closing in for the kill.

* * * *

Kat Dunvegan struggled up from out of a dark pit; a pit shot with pain. Opening her eyes, she had to blink several times before she could focus on what she was seeing. The stars were spinning around her, and her helmet's HUD was blinking on and off. She also felt a fierce pain in her left thigh. This was not good.

With some effort, she got her mind back on track. She remembered the wild maneuvering that had left her moving at a very high closing speed toward one of the

Desotoan cruisers. She also remembered cutting loose with all her ordinance, missiles and guns, at the drive section of the big ship. She didn't know if she'd hit anything, or they'd hit her, but there'd been a big explosion, and then she'd woken up here.

She figured out that the reason things were spinning was that her Viper was pretty much out of control and doing a skewed cartwheel on a ballistic course. But for where? The HUD and other instruments chose that moment to come back online, and Kat set to work analyzing her situation.

The first thing she noticed was a rather large piece of metal sticking out of her leg. There wasn't a lot of bleeding, but she suspected that if she removed the piece of what was very likely part of her spacecraft, she would probably begin bleeding badly.

Stretching behind her hurt like hell, but she was able to reach the first aid kit. With even more pain, she put a pressure bandage all around the wound. Then came the fun part. She had to pull out the metal lance in her leg. The smart bandage she'd used should cover the hole in her leg automatically, but that could be a big "if."

There was nothing else for it. She grasped the metal, pulled it sharply, screamed in agony, and blacked out.

# Chapter 19: Consequences

Although Sun Tzu advised, "On death ground, fight!" Richard Hawke saw no reason to fight the three green-clad Assassins on their own terms.

So as the three ran toward him, shouting something, he turned to the sheer brick wall of the building he stood next to and began to move up the side, just as he had when he'd ambushed the ambushers. The pace for such an ascent was not very fast, but he was out of reach of the three killers before they could get to him. Even better news was that they seemed to be without weapons, perhaps purists who believed that unarmed combat was the be-all and end-all of their art. The Hawkes had no such qualms and used whatever weapons came to hand. Since Richard had no chance to pick up a handy weapon himself, he was quite pleased that the three newcomers were willing to handicap themselves in such a way.

He was halfway up the facade of the office building when shots rang out below. Risking a downward glance, the Hawke brother saw that a security guard had come out of the same building and opened fire with a slug pistol on the three Greenies. The attacker in the middle jerked several times as though he'd been punched, but the bullets didn't stop him, and he quickly closed on the guard. Several quick blows and the uniformed guard dropped to the pavement, clearly dead. As the man's killer looked up at Richard, grinning, the monk turned and resumed his climb to the roof. These guys were apparently bulletproof. And they matched the description of the assassins who had killed the Achaean ruler, Georgios Stephanopolis, two days before.

Richard had some field expedient strangling wire he'd used on the Hamadi squad, but he didn't think it would do him a whole lot of good with these three Greenies, coming after him en masse. He'd have to make do with terrain, tactics, and the Ki of the Hawke clan.

The one who'd been shot suddenly bolted toward the building and leaped, much higher and faster than a normal human. His fingers missed Richard's foot by a good five meters though. Richard turned away and continued his climb. He'd seen the other two run in through the front door. It was a good bet that they would be headed upwards. It would be only polite to greet them properly when they got there.

Flipping himself over the roof cornice, Richard moved quickly to the center of the flat expanse where the openings for a lift and some emergency stairs were in opposite sides of a small structure that housed the machinery for the lift mechanism. He noticed that the master power panel for the lift was to one side of the little building. There were also several pipes and chimneys at various places on the roof, which might have possibilities, but Richard didn't think he had much time to prepare. He'd gone up the side of the building very swiftly, but he was expecting company very shortly. Best to prepare mentally and consider various tactics.

He thought about what he'd seen. The Greenies, whoever they really were or who they represented, were clearly part of the bogus rebellion here on Achaea. They were also at least somewhat bulletproof, extremely fast, and very strong, as evidenced by how the one had killed the security guard with his hands. They also had considerable unarmed combat skills and were trained to use their bodies rather than the usual weapons of assassins or commandos. All in all, they were pretty formidable. Taking one of them out might be difficult, but three at once might be impossible.

Richard had a fleeting thought of Kat and the idea that he might never see her again. But the thought of fleeing didn't enter his mind. These men were evil. They killed indiscriminately. To cap it all off, they had just pissed him off. The Hawkes, despite their profession, were actually about the continuance, even the nurturing of civilization. They were the surgical knife that removed the cancer that might kill the patient.

And these Greenies were clearly the disease. Time to rid the body humankind of this cancer, even if it cost Richard his life.

The lift arrived at the roof, and one of the Greenies rushed out. It looked like they might have split their forces, with one coming up in the lift and at least one other taking the stairs. From their point of view, that not only offered multiple avenues of attach, but it also blocked his escape by those avenues.

The man spied Richard and closed fast. There was no real defense to his attack; it was total offense. He threw a lightning fast punch, but the be-robed monk simply stepped aside and let the blow shatter air next to him. The green-clad man changed direction in a blur of motion and launched a backfist at Richard. Hawke again didn't try to hard-block the blow, but rather slipped it aside with an open hand. He'd begun to suspect that the Greenies were cyborgs, or at least mechanically strengthened, with internal shielding and reflex augmentation, probably picocircuitry based.

But Richard could see from the expression on the man's face, as well as the mean smile the one that had killed the guard downstairs, that these guys were human, and if they were human, they could be killed. He just had to figure out how. As his opponent continued to deliver crushing, rectilinear blows, Richard continued to use soft, circular blocks, deflecting the attacks without trying to meet them directly.

As the blurringly fast combat continued, the monk came up with a couple of theories. With his opponent committed to his next attack, Richard suddenly stopped retreating, and instead stepped inside the next crushingly powerful blow. Richard's hand flashed out, fingers spread and straight. Two of those iron-hard fingers impacted the other man's eyes, and the eyes imploded.

Richard dropped and moved out of the next series of attacks from his opponent, but the new attacks were blind, literally. Suddenly, the Greenie screamed and put his hands to his bleeding sockets as his body finally realized what had happened.

A rush of air behind him warned Richard of another attacker. Hawke spun but took a hard blow to the side of his head. It felt like he'd been hit by an incoming shuttle craft. As much by instinct as anything else, he continued his spin and his green-clad attacker charged by him, missing with a second blow to his head. Richard was slightly groggy, but he'd learned in a hard school. Using his opponent's next charge against him, Hawke redirected the assassin's momentum into a hip throw that sent him headlong into his screaming comrade. The blinded man, thinking he was being attacked, began delivering powerful hand strikes to the head and body of the second Greenie.

A flicker of movement in his peripheral vision drew Richard's attention as the third killer came rushing out of the stairwell.

"Well, shit!" said Richard.

Leaving the other two Greenies to beat the crap out of each other, Richard turned to face his third foe. His head still hurt, and he'd taken a nasty blow to his left shoulder. Nevertheless, years of grueling training under Temujin Hawke had ingrained reflexes of defense and attack to the point that the scion of House Hawke replied to this new attack on an instinctive level.

Like the others, this Greenie wasted no time on subtlety. He was strong, fast, and semi-invulnerable. Why waste around on fancy moves when you're unstoppable?

The incoming attacker did surprise Richard a bit when he leaped into a flying side kick to Richard's head. To a Hawke, flying kicks were for amateurs. They were flashy, and they could be intimidating, he supposed, but they telegraphed from a mile away. Richard just stepped out of the way and punched the man in the groin as he went by. Hmmm. That hurt him.

The Greenie landed in a pained crouch, but he came right back into a kicking attack. His kicks were high. This guy was clearly kick-crazy, and he sought to take Richard out in one dramatic strike, which could happen with a well-placed, powerful kick. Of course, for that stratagem to work, you had to actually hit your target. Richard just backed out of range, maneuvering and looking for an opening to something vital. The representative of the House Hawke backed around the edge of the structure that housed the lift mechanism. He seemed to stumble for a moment, his hand slapping on a bank of large buttons to regain his balance. The deadly dance continued all the way around the structure, passing the open door to the stairs. In a flash, Richard considered and discarded the idea of escaping that way. It might save him or buy him time, but his opponents would still be at large, and he might not be faster than they were anyway. Best to finish things here and now.

As the two fought their way back around to the lift side of the little building, Richard saw what he'd been expecting. The second Greenie had apparently killed or disabled his blinded comrade, and when he saw the monk, he gave a roar of rage. In a flash, Richard disengaged from the kicker and faced Greenie Number Two. Green Two attacked as Richard expected, with a lightning fast straight punch, apparently aiming to take his opponent's head off.

Richard stepped inside the punch and grabbed the man by his punching arm and the collar of his tunic. Richard then sat down, pulling the puncher along with him, but thrusting up into his stomach with his right foot.

The man's face had an almost comical look of surprise before Richard launched him over his head, and right into Kicker. The two green-clad bodies collapsed backwards, right into the lift.

Unfortunately for them, when Richard had stumbled into the controls for the lift, he had slapped the Power switch to Off. The two Greenies' screams could be heard for five stories, followed by a loud crunch.

Richard stood up shakily. He thought he had a concussion, and his left shoulder was definitely damaged, perhaps dislocated. His right knee hurt too. He should be able to limp to the nearest aid station, though. The Greenies wouldn't be going anywhere.

* * * *

In another part of the city of Mycenae, office life continued more or less as normal.

Nikos was still half asleep as he refilled his coffee cup for the third time that morning. He'd just come out of a terminally boring meeting, where nothing but bitching had been accomplished. For Christ's sake, you'd think that one of those complainers would come up with a solution to their problems. But, no. All they did was whine and complain, and expect everybody else to come up with the fixes for their imagined problems, most of which they'd created for themselves.

Nikos just wished something interesting would happen around this place. Maybe that would wake him up.

As Nikos stepped out of the coffee mess, there was a horrific crashing sound, and the outside wall at the far end of the hall imploded, throwing bricks and building material in his direction. Nikos jumped back into the doorway of the coffee room just as a large metal object came hurtling by, narrowly missing crushing him.

After a few more moments, and when nothing else came flying at him, and the crashing noises had subsided, Nikos set down his coffee cup and went into what remained of the hall to see what had happened. Not too far from him, the metal object had come to a halt, having smashed into a load-bearing pillar, which thankfully hadn't collapsed. As the Achaean office worker approached the metal tube, he realized it looked like a fighter spacecraft that he'd had a model of when he was a kid. A very beat-up fighter spacecraft at that.

Approaching cautiously, he jumped back when the canopy slid back, shedding plaster, plastic, and pieces of brick. When nothing else moved, Nikos edged closer. When he could see into the cockpit, what he saw was a beautiful young woman. She'd apparently managed to remove her helmet, but now she was just sitting there, panting. And there was blood. A lot of blood. It painted the inside of the pilot's compartment.

The pilot looked up at him, smiled, and saluted. She said, "Captain Katerina Dunvegan, reporting for duty."

Then she passed out.

# Chapter 20: Next Steps

"Mister Hawke, we're being challenged by the Achaean Navy," said Scott Douglas, Gwendolyn's pilot.

Roland Hawke had been studying some of the CI intel regarding the Alamut Sector, since he figured they'd be heading that way very soon. Scottie's call snapped him back to the now. He responded,"Is that usual?"

Scott's response was laconic. "Not really, but I gather from the news feeds that there was a major naval action with a Desotoan task force here just yesterday. Our sensors are picking up a lot of debris from what I suspect used to be spacecraft. I'm guessing these local Achaean lads are just a tad paranoid at this point."

Jason and Roland looked at each other. Jason said, "Not a coincidence, I'd wager."

Roland nodded. "Not if the Desotoans are involved. This may put a whole new complexion on the assassination attempts and the employment of the Hashishiyun. It may also put a different slant on our mission."

"It's a power grab, designed to play on the chaos after the assassination of the Moderator."

Scottie spoke over the ship comm. "Apparently, someone did assassinate the Achaean President and several high-ranking government types dirtside in the capital city of Mycenae. They say it was some guys dressed in green."

Roland frowned. "It figures. I guess we're a bit late here."

Jason gave him a grim smile. "But we might still be able to pick up the trail of the assassins."

Roland nodded. "Scottie, get us dirt-side as soon as you can."

"Aye-aye, Sir!"

Jason gave a wry smile and said, "You know, it irritates me to have to call these Greenies assassins. We were brought up to think of assassination as a worthy profession; a bit like a surgical military strike. But when I think of these Hashishiyun, I don't get that vibe at all. They are nothing more than killers for hire. And for hire to the Desotoans, at that."

Roland smiled in turn. “I know exactly what you’re talking about. I feel the same way. But there are those who would see House Hawke as exactly the same breed. I think they’re wrong, but you know that’s what people think.”

“Which makes the fact that the Hawkes have always kept a low profile seem like a really good idea.”

“That it is. That it is.”

* * * *

Eight hours later, they landed at the main spaceport for Achaea.

The news of the assassination and the space battle was everywhere. And the mood of the Achaeans was fierce. They had a good idea of what the Desotoans were trying, and they did not like it.

Roland and Jason had stopped for cup of tea. They were watching a news feed on the holo-receiver on their table.

Roland said, “You know, I think this business might backfire big time on the Desotoans, even if they do succeed in putting boots on the ground. These people are pissed!”

“Yeah,” replied his brother, “and the Greeks have a long history of rebellion against aggressive invaders.”

Roland nodded. “Well, they may get their chance again. I doubt this is the last card in the Desotoans’ hand.”

Jason fiddled with the mini-comp on the table.

“And speaking of cards, I’m doing a search on Kat and Richard.” His eyes widened a bit. “Oops! Looks like both are in the hospital on the local Confed Navy base.”

"Both are in the hospital? I guess they might like wild sex, but that seems a bit extreme." He thought for a moment. "I guess I could see Kat in the 'wild sex' part, but Richard? I mean, he's a monk!"

Jason chuckled and said, "Maybe he's making up for lost time."

He looked down at the display.

"According to this, Kat was out there doing something heroic in the battle with the Desotoans, and some witnesses swear that Richard took out three of our Green friends by himself." He read a bit further. "He may have added some rebel snipers to his bag as well." Jason looked up at his brother. "I guess they've both been kind of busy."

"So it probably wasn't sex that landed them in the hospital."

"Or not only sex. Let's go ask them."

* * * *

Like hospital rooms elsewhere, Richard Hawke's room was bland and smelt of chemicals. It was also empty.

Jason said, "My money says he's over in Kat's room."

Roland smiled and nodded. "No bet. Let's try there."

After some inquiries, and making their way through the maze of corridors, the two Hawkes found the correct room. Richard was indeed there, sitting next to what they assumed was Kat's bed. At least Jason figured it was Kat. The figure on the bed was covered in bandages and encased in a reconstructive bubble. Clearly, her injuries had been quite extensive.

Richard stood as they entered the room. He moved a bit stiffly, and he had flexible immobilizers on both his left shoulder and his right leg.

"Wow!" said Roland, "They really beat the crap out of you!"

He gave a wicked grin. "Didn't Dad teach your any better?'

Richard gave his own lopsided grin. "Apparently not. So what brings you two derelicts to sunny Achaea? Sightseeing?"

Jason replied, "If I were going sightseeing, Achaea is most definitely not the place I'd go. No, we're on the trail of some green-clad Hashishiyun. Looks like you found them first."

He gave his brother an exaggerated once-over. "Or they found you."

"A little bit of both, I think," said Richard. "I went looking for members of a fake local rebellion. I did find some of the so-called rebels, but I also found a bunch of Bishtian commandos, and, of course, our Green friends." He assumed a beatific expression. "Both groups have gone to meet their karma, I suppose. Perhaps they'll be reincarnated as lice or something else small and nasty."

Roland laughed.

"Jason and I have done our bit to rid the galaxy of such vermin as well." He turned to Jason. "So, I'm thinking it's time for us to pay a visit to Alamut."

Jason nodded. "Yeah, they should most definitely be next on our list." He turned to his other brother. "Richard, how about you? Do you feel up to a little trip?"

Richard sobered. "Not this time, guys. I want to be around when Kat comes out of her medically-induced coma, and besides, I've got this feeling."

Jason raised his eyebrows. "A feeling? A feeling like there might be more Hashishiyun around?"

The monk shook his head. "No, not them. I think something big and nasty is headed this way."

Roland was thoughtful. "More Desotoans?"

Richard shrugged. "Maybe. In any event, I think I should stay. You two can go be heroes."

Jason snorted. "Yeah, right. Well, you take care brother."

"And you two, as well."

## Chapter 21: Move and Countermove

"Do we have any new intel from Rear Admiral Garcia as to the situation in the Achaean System?" asked Admiral de Ulloa. "The last we heard, the task force had just shipped out. There's been nothing since. It would be nice to know what we're sailing into."

The Desotoan Empire's Tenth Fleet chief intelligence officer, Captain Federico Ollarsaba, nodded distractedly. He was studying the holo-globe map of the Achaean System and looking for possible inroads and weak points. Of course, they'd all been doing just that for the last two weeks, but until they broke out of hyperspace in that system, this would all remain theoretical. Ollarsaba, like his boss, de Ulloa, liked to have as many optional plans as possible.

The whole plan hinged upon the task force being successful. All the intel feeds indicated a huge disparity of forces with most of the power on the Desotoan side. Once the "rebel fleet" from Achaea had been disposed of, de Ulloa's fleet could take over as a peacekeeping force, to stabilize the Achaean System in the wake of their rebellion. Of course, the Desotoans would have no plans of ever leaving the system, and with such a sizable naval force in the area, the annexation of Achaea would be a fait accompli in the face of any protests from the Confederation.

Ollarsaba turned to the admiral. "Don Juan, we have received no additional information from either the task force or Naval Intelligence. I hate to admit it, but I'm afraid we're going in fairly blind."

Ollarsaba very much disliked having to say that. Admiral Juan de Ulloa was from one of the most powerful houses in the Desotoan Empire, and his political appointment to the post of Commander of Tenth Fleet had resulted in many promotions among his sycophants, Ollarsaba included. The good news was that de Ulloa accepted such shameless sucking up as his due, rather than as a means to someone else's end. It coincided with his entire life and the life of a noble of the De Soto Empire. But it was because of this arrangement that his fleet intel chief was really hesitant to admit that he didn't know anything new.

As a CYA measure, Ollarsaba added, "Admiral, maybe we can light a fire under those pogues back at

Fleet Intelligence. I can't do a whole lot if they give me no information."

"True. True." De Ulloa had never been a great thinker, but he knew court politics backwards and forwards. "Draft a demand for the latest intelligence for my signature. We will not be left swinging in the breeze by those rear echelon idiots! And copy the Emperor. That should motivate them to get their asses in gear."

"Aye-aye, Don Juan!"

* * * *

Captain Joe Fuchida entered Admiral Ghormley's office with some hard-copy reports in hand. "Admiral, we have new reports from the Achaean System. It's not good."

Ghormley gave a tired smile and replied, "Is it ever? So what have you got?"

"A Desotoan task force composed of two cruisers and four destroyers entered the Achaean System two days ago. They said that they were there to protect Desotoan citizens in the face of the Achaean rebellion. And they also said that they were there at the request of the Achaean government."

"Ah, the Big Lie, so near and dear to the hearts of the Dons! So what do we know? Was there any action?"

"Yes, Sir. According to our dispatches, the Achaeans took a pretty bad mauling, but they totally destroyed the Desotoan task force. The Achaean local space forces were aided considerably by the squadron of Confed fighters we left behind." He paused, and then laughed.

The admiral looked at him quizzically. "What about this situation is funny?"

Fuchida sobered a bit, but still retained a bit of a smile. "Admiral, do you remember those ASP boats you left behind, figuring they were useless?"

Ghormley rolled his eyes. "Okay. I'm guessing they did something right."

"That they did, Sir. They took out at least two destroyers and may have gotten an assist in destroying one of the cruisers. Yes, Sir. I'd say they did something right."

Ghormley displayed a wry grin.

"Hey, I'll admit I might have been wrong there. Nevertheless, it sounds like we need to set course back for Achaea. I'm concerned about leaving this sector open, though." He thought for a minute."All right then. We'll leave one carrier and all the cruisers here. But we'll take the battlewagons and the other carrier with us to Achaea. I strongly suspect that the Desotoans have more surprises in store than that one task force."

"Yes, Sir. Do you want me to call the staff?"

"Good idea. Get them over here in about an hour. We're going to want to crunch some numbers." He chuckled. "And hopefully some Desotoans."

## Chapter 22: Scenic Climes

Cadiz was a lovely planet. It was green and lush, and it was a hub of merchant shipping for the sector. A major crossroads for various galactic trade routes, it was a rich planet, a jewel in the crown of the human-inhabited planets of the galaxy.

It was also close the heart of the Desotoan Empire, a fact of which Cuchulain Hawke was all too aware. When he'd run the trace on Petrov's FTL call, he'd gotten a location here in the heart of the Empire. This was, to say the least, highly suggestive that the source of the orders to kill off the Hawke Clan was of Desotoan origins. And it was that source that Koo was looking for. It was time to teach someone that screwing the Hawkes was career-limiting, not to mention the key to a much shorter life span.

Keying in his personal mini-comp to the planetary net, Koo first identified and nullified the inevitable tracers on his searches. Such tracers could be from the net service suppliers, the government, both local and Empire, or just hackers. There was a good chance that all three sources would seek knowledge of anyone using the planetary net, but the Hawkes spent money wisely in arming their personal comps with all the latest stealth tech. Koo was electronically invisible. Any system can be cracked, of course, but not in the small amount of time he'd be doing his searches.

The call had originated from Espiritu Santo, the main spaceport for the planet of Cadiz, where Cuchulain had made planetfall.

"Convenient," Koo muttered to himself.

Espiritu was also the most populous city on the planet, so it took some moments for the tracer to find its source; in a large office building at the far end of the city from the spaceport itself.

"Not so convenient," he grumbled.

As the youngest Hawke signaled to a local transport, he caught a flash of movement out of the corner of his eye, which caused him to fade into the shadows instinctively. Without seeming to, he checked out whatever it was that had drawn his attention. His jaw almost dropped when he saw his erstwhile crush, Gemma Jackson, standing outside of the Arrivals gates.

As he watched, an expensive looking ground-effect car pulled up and she got in, and he watched as the car pulled out into traffic.

"Now that is not likely to be a coincidence," he thought.

If it wasn't a coincidence, then it meant that the lovely Gemma was an agent. An agent for whom was the big question. She could be Desotoan, or she could be Confed. There were other powers out there as well. But none of them would be likely to aid him in his mission. Quite the contrary.

Too bad. Back to the mission.

Koo hailed a ground taxi and requested a location about a mile from the office building that was his objective, as he had identified in his search.

In short order, the young man exited the taxi and began a casual-seeming walk toward Cortez Torre, Cortez Tower, a two-hundred story office building on the east side of Espiritu Santo.

Young Hawke took his time and completely circled the building, reflecting that only a civilization with sophisticated technology could have built such an edifice. But even such a civilization, as interpreted by the Desotoans, apparently did not feel it odd to build one so gaudy. The multiple facets of the permaglass windows were interspersed with garish murals depicting gigantic merchants and soldiers of the De Soto Empire. There was also a lot of gold leaf. A lot of gold leaf. Koo knew that gold didn't have the same value it once had, but it was still valuable, and this place had been decorated with it in abundance.

Hawke entered the Tower after completely circumnavigating the huge building once and observing it from a small restaurant across the street for some time. The call he'd traced had come from some outfit called Galaxy Imports, which was a front organization if he'd ever heard of one.

Just as he was getting ready to leave his observation post at the little restaurant, Gemma Jackson had shown up at the front entrance of Cortez Torre. What looked like the same ritzy car dropped her off. Koo noted that she was now wearing a form-fitting business suit that pressed the limits of businesslike and sexual suggestiveness. And she wore it well. The young scion of House Hawke admired expertise when he saw it. And other things. But, to business.

He gave Gemma some time to clear the lobby, and then the young Hawke entered Cortez Torre. He was casual and dressed moderately well. Well enough to not look like a street person, but not well enough to be noticed as some wealthy mover and shaker. The goal was basic invisibility, and Koo did it well. Strolling casually, but not dawdling, a man with a goal in mind, he found the directory for the offices in the building. As he had ascertained from his net search, Galaxy Imports occupied the top five floors of the Tower. Koo keyed in a lift for the one hundred and ninetieth floor. He would actually have preferred to come in through the roof, since Hawke doctrine preferred starting at the top, but Koo wasn't planning on clearing the building. He was only looking for one man, and some information.

Exiting the lift at the 190th floor, Koo immediately moved down the plush corridor to the emergency stairwell at the east end. Presumably, there was an identical exit on the west. Even the most sophisticated technologies failed sometimes, and building codes required alternate routes for emergency egress. Maintenance folks also used the stairwells at times, and there were frequently limited access doors in the stairwells so that they could work on the building's infrastructure.

That was what Koo was looking for now, and he found it on a landing outside the 196th floor. The lock was rudimentary, at least by Hawke standards, and in a moment, he was inside the walls of the enemy's citadel.

Of course, the Tower Security people had considered such an invasion method, and they had taken some measures to secure the infrastructure against this. Two things worked against Security and in Koo's favor. For one thing, Koo had trained in the Hawke school of covert ingress, and he had sophisticated tools and the expertise to use them whenever necessary. The other thing that helped him out also gave him a quiet (very quiet) chuckle. The Maintenance types had apparently considered the security devices a pain to work around, so they'd cheated most of them. Afterwards, they either forgot to remove the cheats or just left them in place for the next time.

Koo had to move upwards five floors first, which took some time. That was okay; he wasn't on a tight schedule. In fact, for snipers and assassins, patience could well be considered the cardinal virtue. Take your time, do the job right, and un-ass safely and preferably invisibly. In the cases where his Tower Maintenance friends had not cheated the security devices, Koo did so now, moving slowly but surely, first up to the top floor, and then across the ceilings to the place where she saw the most comm connections. That would be the nerve center, and close to the center of power.

It had taken him the better part of two hours to move into his current position, but now Koo was able to maneuver a snoop down into the room below him. Once he had reached the top floor, he had transitioned from the walls to the ceilings, that route providing the most accessible path to where he wanted to go. Now his microsnoop hovered on its own picotech antigravity field over the room below. Sure enough, the room was festooned with holo displays and other telltales, keeping the Galaxy Imports command apprised of all the latest security info as well as supplying real time data about the world around them. Hell, it might be tapped into the FTL interstellar feeds for all he knew. The setup was clearly very sophisticated.

Unfastening the catches that held the roof panels in place, Koo dropped silently to the floor. Neither tech heard him. They were both totally immersed in their data links. The youngest Hawke brother noticed silver plates on the temples of the techs. So, they were metalheads; able to access the data feeds directly through terminal buds embedded in their cortexes. The Hawkes considered such body and brain mods as abominations. The whole Hawked philosophy was based on using the organic human body and mind to its fullest. metalheads and cyborgs were anathema to the clan.

There was a reasonable chance that neither tech would even notice him entering and leaving the room, but a “reasonable chance” just didn’t cut it for the Hawkes. Moving smoothly and swiftly, Koo glided up behind the tech closest to him and with one well-aimed, stiffened finger, hit a nerve ganglion in the man’s neck. The tech dropped off his chair onto the floor. The second tech may have seen the movement out of the corner of his eye, for he began to turn his head in the direction of his colleague. But Koo was on him too quickly for him to react. In a moment, the second metalhead joined his partner on the floor.

These two were no physical threat. The most the techs could have done was raise an alarm. No need to kill them. And now Koo had secured not only the information flow into and out of the Tower, but he had also assured himself of at least one path of retreat for when he needed to exfiltrate this place.

Koo readied the dart guns on the back of his hands. They were virtually invisible to even a trained eye, but could deliver chems or toxins that would result in shock, unconsciousness, or death. Moving through the only door, Koo found himself in a security office. Rather than the data feeds of the metalheads, the holos in this office showed the approaches to the Galaxy Imports office complex with several displaying the approaches to all four sides of the Cortez Torre.

Too bad they didn't show the door from the tech room. Too bad for the guards, at least.

Koo was loaded with narco-darts this time. These two might be physical threats, but they would be out of it for at least an hour now. He ejected the narco magazines and loaded with darts that would inject a fast-acting, lethal neurotoxin. There would be no playing around and no mercy now. He was getting too close to his designated target.

Moving on, Hawke opened a door that led to a main corridor with armed guards at both ends. It was roughly twenty yards to each guard, and Koo didn't hesitate. De-focusing his eyes and extending his Ki senses, he stepped out into the corridor, arms straight out to either side.

Phut. Phut. The dart guns on the back of his hands released their cartridges of compressed gas, and two darts filled with deadly neurotoxin flashed across the intervening distances. One guard took his in the throat. The other, perhaps with faster reflexes, began to drop into a shooting crouch, raising his plasma pistol. Because he had crouched, the dart took him in the eye instead of the throat. He dropped even faster than his partner. Both guards were dead, the bioengineered nerve poison shutting down their nervous systems, and ultimately their brains, virtually instantaneously. Once the darts hit them, they were pretty much dead. Their plasma pistols would have made a lot more noise, but they were no more deadly.

Koo chose to explore the door to his right. If he were oriented correctly, that would take him toward the outer corner of the building. Large, windowed offices seemed a likely base of operations for whoever ran this organization.

As he silently entered the next office, Hawke heard a scream of pain. He didn't allow that to cause him to overreact, but he thought it might have been Gemma. Of course, if it was indeed Gemma, the scream could mean any of a number of things. A falling out. The discovery of her as an agent. Possibly even rough sex, although it would have taken extremely rough sex to elicit a scream like that. In the proper time, he would find out, but he wouldn't be rushed. These things had their own timing.

Taking a deep, cleansing breath, Koo approached the door that the scream had come from. Time for the big show. The door was locked, but that didn't last long, and when it opened, he was ready.

Hawke took in the scene in a glance. Two bruisers were leaning over a figure apparently tied to a chair, and the tied person was Gemma Jackson. There was a lean, sinister-looking man in an expensive suit standing not far away, and there was another man in an even more expensive suit sitting casually at a huge desk across the room. He seemed mildly interested, even amused by the proceedings.

Koo wasted no time in darting the two thugs, who dropped in their tracks. The one he'd tagged as Mister Sinister went for a shoulder holster, but Koo was on him before he could bring the pistol up. The young Hawke grabbed the man's hand with the pistol still in it, and smashed the gun against the man's forehead repeatedly. Mister Sinister's eyes rolled up in his head and he collapsed, unconscious.

The last man, and the most well dressed, made a dash for a door on the opposite side of the room. Koo used a throwing knife this time, and took the man in the back of the right knee. The guy screamed in pain and dropped to the lush carpet. Hawke moved quickly to the fallen man's side and struck him in a nerve ganglion in the back of his neck. The exec collapsed, unconscious.

Now Koo turned back to Gemma. She was bleeding and bruised, but it looked like they hadn't been working on her for long. She looked more furious than hurt. He stopped and looked down at her.

She snarled, "Well, aren't you going to get me out of these bindings?"

Koo assumed a relaxed posture and said, "I'm not sure. That could depend on how you answer this question. Who are you really?"

She glared at him and strained at her bonds. No luck. With obvious reluctance, she grated out, "My name really is Gemma Jackson. I work for Confed Central Intelligence."

"And why are you here?"

"That's classified!"

"Cool. Have a nice day." He turned to go.

"Wait! All right. I was following up a lead regarding the assassination attempt on the Moderator. The lead brought me here."

Koo had heard about the assassination attempt, of course. It was all over the holo-faxes. Now, he put two and two together. That team who had tried to kill his family was there to recruit the Hawkes. It was only after Temujin had refused the offer that they had called in the hit on the Hawke compound. The two attempts most likely came from the same source.

Kneeling, he used the throwing knife he'd removed from the executive's leg to cut Gemma's bonds. Of course, he gave her no opening to strike him. No sense being a total idiot.

Once he'd helped her to her feet, he nodded towards the two unconscious men. "So who are these guys, and who's picking up their tab?"

She gave them a hard look.

"As near as I can tell, they're working for Desotoan Intelligence." She pointed at the unconscious exec. "His name is Edouardo Lopez. He's been known to work for Don Juan Balboa, head of Desotoan Security."

He cocked his head at the others. "And these are all his flunkies?"

She nodded. “Yes. I don’t know what gave me away, but they were waiting for me. I don’t think they knew I was Confed, but they clearly knew that I was an agent. I walked into a trap.”

Koo nodded. “Okay. Let’s wake up sleeping beauty over there and see what else he knows.”

She gave a very nasty smile. “Oh yeah, I’m going to enjoy that!”

# Chapter 23: Alamut

Scott Douglas brought Gwendolyn into a stealthy, geosynchronous orbit over the northern continent of the planet Alamut. On the run in from their insertion point, he'd picked up numerous sensor traces designed to alert the locals to any visitors, welcome of unwelcome. Since he and the Hawkes hadn't been invited, Scottie decided to go totally covert. After all, when you're crashing a party, you want it to be a surprise.

Scott's ship, Gwendolyn, actually carried quite a bit of military-grade armament, but she certainly wasn't equipped to take on an entire planet. That left subterfuge and stealth, both of which were familiar stratagems for Scottie and the Hawkes.

Scott set all the necessary alarms and left Gwendolyn to keeping watch. Then he joined Roland and Jason in the small wardroom/lunchroom/meeting room.

The pilot said, "Well, we're here. Now what?"

Roland smiled and held up a data marble. "Central Intelligence gave us some information about Alamut, including a contact on the surface."

Jason looked at him sharply. "A contact? A CI agent?"

Roland shook his head. "Nope. This person is a leader of the local resistance movement."

Scottie said, "With a planet full of assassins, I shouldn't think any resistance movement would be possible."

Jason looked thoughtful and replied, "I studied all the intel we have on this place, and Alamut is not actually a planet-full of assassins. The assassins are concentrated around a Citadel complex-cum-palace in the mountains on the northern continent. I guess the boss likes to have them ready to hand. The rest of the planet is a bunch of farmers, fisherman, and merchants, pretty much like anyplace else."

Scott said, "So, who is this contact guy?"

Roland chuckled. "This guy is a girl by the name of Ciera Sultana."

Jason's eyes widened a bit. "A girl?"

Roland shrugged. "Hey, she's survived in a resistance movement on a planet like this for several years. I'd guess she's very competent, and smart."

Scott looked sour. "And probably with a face like a shovel."

"Maybe."

* * * *

Because they were dropping from the high stratosphere, the Hawkes decided to go with grav sleds rather than parachutes. The sleds had their own air supply, albeit a somewhat limited one, and they could take the reentry heat better. It still wouldn't be fun, but the Hawkes had trained in a hard school.

They did a pre-drop check of each other's harness and weapons, making sure everything was well secured and that nothing had been forgotten.

Jason, the former Marine, carried a disassembled sniper rifle in his pack, along with .75 caliber ammo. The rifle was an older design, actually what the grunts called a "smoke pole," using actual, albeit extremely sophisticated, gunpowder to propel its slugs. Older design or not, the gun could take out a sentry at three clicks or more, and Jason was expert in its use.

Roland carried a smaller combat carbine with smart munitions. With it, once the round had been locked on through the smart sight, he could kill a target no matter how much the bad guy might jink or run. It could also be fired around corners with the gunsight feed running directly to a HUD in Roland's helmet. You could run from such a weapon, but you'd only die tired.

Both brothers also carried an assortment of edged weapons. Roland preferred knives and a wakizashi, while Jason packed shuriken and a katana. The Hawke clan was trained in all kinds of weapons, but each had his own preferences. Having said that, any one of them could pick up an enemy's weapon and use it expertly, the way natural musicians can play an instrument almost as soon as picking it up. The Hawkes were virtuosos of the battlefield.

Scott's voice came over their comm channel. "Coming up on insertion point. Three. Two. One. Drop!"

A revolving bay in Gwendolyn's belly rolled, and first Roland then Jason were ejected into the ship's powerful slipstream. They dropped quickly, well into the planet's gravity well. Both were expert at this sort of drop, and they quickly oriented themselves toward the primary LZ, even though it was currently far outside of visual range. GPS and the maps loaded into the sleds' little brains showed the brothers exactly where they were in relation to the landing zone and to each other. Low-energy passive sensors monitored the atmosphere for possible threats. The drop looked clear.

The sleds were extremely stealthy, virtually invisible to even the most sophisticated sensors. That didn't mean they were comfortable, however. Since they were so light, there was considerable buffeting as they went down through the atmosphere. Heat shields bled most of the built-up heat away from the occupants, but there was no question in Jason's mind that if it weren't for the heat shields, he and Roland would be crispy critters.

But all things come to an end, and so did their flight. The small onboard computers zeroed in on their designated LZ, and the sleds came to a bit of a bumpy landing on a level plain in some small mountains. Make that "fairly level plain," thought Jason as he bled off his forward motion by hitting a fairly large boulder. There was a crashing, tearing sound, and the next thing he knew, he was airborne, minus his sled.

Jason had endured many parachute drops and ziplines, so he knew to tuck and roll. In the process, he found several other large rocks that objected to his disturbing their slumbers.

Finally, he came to a somewhat bruised halt. Jason moved all his limbs carefully. Okay, nothing irreparably broken. Slowly, and a bit painfully, he stood up and checked out his surroundings. Roland was exiting his completely undamaged sled, looking like he'd stepped off a recruiting poster for special ops soldiers. Fifty yards beyond Roland, Jason saw a small figure clad in desert robes pointing a large bore rifle at them.

Jason held up his hands and said, "We're friends!" More quietly, he added, "I hope."

A surprisingly sweet woman's voice said, "You're CI?"

Roland replied, "Not exactly."

Jason added, "We're Hawkes."

The woman didn't lower her gun. "And what's a Hawke?"

Roland gave a small smile. “We’re problem solvers.”

She asked, “And what problem are you here to solve?”

Jason answered, “The Hashishiyun.”

She lowered the cloth that had covered her face. Jason could see that she was blond and blue-eyed, with a snub nose. She was also quite tall for a woman, and lean-muscled.

She nodded. “Good. The Hashishiyun are a problem that needs to be solved. My name is Ciera Sultana. Together, we shall kill many Hashishiyun!”

# Chapter 24: Hashishiyun

"Come," Ciera Sultana said, "I have transportation."

She led the brothers over a nearby rise and toward what appeared to be a pile of dirt. Upon closer inspection, it proved to be a ground effect vehicle. A very dirty ground effect vehicle.

Ciera looked back at them deadpan. "It doesn't reflect light, and it's well camouflaged when stationary. My father always believed in making nature work for us."

Jason chuckled and said, "He sounds like our Dad."

She gave him a quizzical look. "You are brothers?"

Roland gave a wry smile and replied, "I hate to admit it at times, but yes, we're brothers. I'm Roland Hawke, and this is my big galoot of a brother, Jason."

She nodded, still serious. “I used to have brothers. The Old Man had them all killed.”

That put an end to that conversation.

They all climbed into the backcountry vehicle, and Sultana set off over the hardpan desert towards the distant mountains.

After some time, Roland asked, “So why did the Old Man on the Mountain have your family killed?”

She was silent for a long moment, and Roland thought she might not answer. But then she said, “My father spoke out against the Assassins. He was a carpenter, a very good one, but no one would trade with us because of the threat of the Hashishiyun. My father told the people of our town that the Assassins had served a useful purpose at one time, but now they were only holding our world back from free trade with other planets.”

She paused for another long moment. “I was away at my aunt’s. When I returned, my father, my mother, and both my brothers were dead. The Assassins burnt our house to the ground and nailed up a proclamation in the towns saying, ‘So dies anyone who defies the Old Man of the Mountains.’

“I was thirteen, but it was on that day that I joined the Resistance.” She was silent for some time again, but then she went on. “My family were among the first colonists here. In the early days, it may be true that Alamut only retained its independence because of the Hashishiyun, but that time is long past. This is a poor world. If we are to develop at all, we need to become part of the galactic community, to modernize, and to move beyond the bad old days."

Jason was thoughtful. "You know, that doesn't always work out all that well. It's my understanding that Alamut has few natural resources. Modernization takes money, and lots of it. All I'm saying is that it might be more difficult than you think to change your planet."

She nodded. "Oh, I know all that. But if we never try, we'll never know if we can succeed, will we? Besides, there has never been any resource exploration here. We locals can't afford it, and the Assassins make sure that no one else comes in and does it for us. They are paranoid that if natural resources are found, then the planet will be invaded. Never mind that everyone here might be better off."

Roland was thoughtful. "So most of the money that does come in goes to them?"

She nodded, never taking her eyes off the rough track they were traversing. The track was leading them in a winding path up into the craggy mountains. "There is a very small amount of trade. However, most of the profits and most of the technology and equipment goes to the Hashishiyun. The rest of us eke out a poor living from hardscrabble farming and minor trade."

Jason thought about that for a few minutes. "It sounds like the Hashishiyun were born out of the necessity to keep the world free, but over time they've become the overlords that they once fought to repel."

Ciera nodded, never taking her eyes off the faint track in front of her. “It is as you say. They have become rich parasites, sucking the lifeblood of this world for their own betterment, while the rest of the planet languishes in poverty.”

Jason gave a grim chuckle.

“Well, let’s see what we can do about that.” He focused in the distance ahead of them and said, “Miss Sultana, stop please. I believe I see our first customers up ahead.”

The resistance fighter didn’t comment. She just pulled the vehicle off the track and behind some nearby boulders. The three got out of the vehicle and moved forward carefully.

Roland looked over the edge of a large rock, using his mini-binocs to spy out what his brother had spotted. Jason had always had freakishly sharp eyes, so it didn’t surprise Roland that he’d been the first one to see any threat.

Roland sat back down behind the boulder and commented, “Okay, we have two presumed hostiles up ahead. I don’t see a vehicle, so its either concealed, or they were dropped off.”

Jason nodded. “It’s probably a picket. They most likely have to report in periodically to assure the head of the guard detachment that all is well.”

Ciera gave a grim smile. “But all is not well. However, I know from past reconnaissance in this area that the pickets are slack. There is nothing to see, and nothing ever happens. They do not report in as regularly as they probably should, and the ones that are posted in these remote locations are not exactly the first string of the Hashishiyun."

Jason laughed. "Ah, they're shitbirds."

Roland chuckled and Ciera looked puzzled. She said, "Shitbirds?"

Jason nodded. "An old Marine Corps term for incompetent, lazy, or shiftless troops."

She nodded. "Yes. They are indeed shitbirds."

Roland said, "And shitbirds are in season."

Jason unloaded his rifle from their vehicle. "I'm up for this one."

Roland nodded. He looked over the boulders. "I make it as two thousand meters."

Jason nodded silently and dialed the range into his sight. Then, he took a standing stance, resting the his left hand on one of the large rocks, with his right hand on the weapon's action. He looked at the targets through the sight. Both pickets were visible from here. Very poor tradecraft on their part.

He took a deep breath, released half of it, and squeezed the trigger. The rifle bucked, and he shifted to the other target. Again, a deep breath, release, and squeeze. A muffled crack came from the weapon.

Roland, watching through his binocs, said, "Both targets down. No more movement."

He turned to Ciera. "Let's get moving. Places to go. People to kill."

# Chapter 25: The Second Fleet

Senior Petty Officer Jim Wilson came into the office of Lieutenant Commander James Lewis and said, "Skipper, we've got sensor readings on another Desotoan fleet entering the system."

"Well, shit," replied Lewis, "Okay, let's get the boys and girls saddled up. Are all boats online?"

Wilson nodded. "More or less. ASP Three took a pretty good hit from a plasma cannon, but the maintenance crews have been working around the clock, and her commander says she's ready to go."

Lewis put on his cover and they headed out the door toward the ASP squadron area. "Cool. Do we have any hard numbers on this new bunch of hostiles yet?"

"Yes, Sir, and it doesn't look good."

Lewis gave him a sidelong glance and said, “Well, don’t be coy, Guns. What are we facing?”

“It looks like two battlewagons, four cruisers, and about ten destroyers, Sir.”

Lewis frowned. “Well, we are well and truly fucked. Do the Greeks and the fighter jocks have the same intel?”

“Yes, Sir. Actually, we got it from some Achaean picket boats.”

They came up to the boat area, which was swarming with men, getting ready to head out, into harm’s way.

Lewis nodded, half to himself, and then he muttered, “Well, now we get to earn our princely salaries, yet again.”

* * * *

Lieutenant Colonel Gareth Blaustein was donning his flight suit and examining the latest intel estimates on a screen on the wall when the door opened. He didn’t look over, but continued to examine the take from the system sensors.

Then a voice behind him said, “Captain Katerina Dunvegan reporting for duty, Sir.”

Startled, he turned around. It was indeed Kat. He looked her over, and noticed she seemed to be favoring her left side a bit. He said, “Last I heard, you were in the hospital.” He gave her a hard look.“And you do look a bit worse for wear. Besides, you broke that bird I gave you.”

She gave a shrug, and then winced. "Sorry about the bird, Skipper. But you should have seen the other guy!"

He grinned. "Actually, I did see the other guy. And what possessed you to do a kamikaze run on that cruiser?"

"Sir, that was totally an accident. I got caught in a blast wave, and the next thing I knew, I was flying up the keester of the Desotoan cruiser. I was reminded of that old Navy axiom, 'When in doubt, attack!' Besides, if I'd tried to run, they would have blown me out of space. So I went for it."

"You did indeed. And that cruiser is now toast. Are you sure you're up to flying status though?"

"I hear there are a bunch of bad guys out there, Sir. I want a piece of them."

He grinned again. "Well, as it happens, I have freshly patched up bird, but I'm short one fighter pilot. Think you can do it?"

She snapped to attention. "Yes, Sir!"

He gave her a wry smile. "But no more suicide runs, okay?"

"Aye-aye, Sir!" In a low voice to herself, she muttered, "Hopefully."

Blaustein asked, "What was that?"

"Oh, nothing."

* * * *

Admiral Juan de Ulloa marshaled his fleet at the edge of the Achaean system. It was a fairly large battle group, and the ships had come out of hyperspace scattered over millions of miles. This was not entirely a bad thing, because it obviated the possibility of collisions. De Ulloa hated to admit it, but the Desotoan hyperspace sensors weren't as sophisticated as those of the Confederation, so it was wise to err on the side of caution when the ships' sensors couldn't see each other very clearly. Trying to keep too tight a formation through hyper could result in the unnecessary loss of warships that he might need.

Of course, if the intelligence estimates were correct, he should still have overwhelming force against the paltry and outdated Achaean fleet, if fleet it could truly be called. A squadron, more likely.

Speaking of intelligence. "Send Captain Ollarsaba to the bridge."

About five minutes later, the fleet intelligence officer appeared on the flag bridge and came to attention before the admiral. Saluting, he barked, "Captain Ollarsaba reporting, sir!"

De Ulloa made a calming motion with his hand. "At ease Captain. What is the latest intel take on Achaea, and have we heard anything from the task force?"

"Admiral, I have received no new information from Naval Intelligence. And, more disturbingly, we have not received any communications from the task force, either. Either they are too busy to report, or they have been wiped out completely."

The admiral looked thoughtful. The truth was, he had no idea what to do next. "I seriously doubt they are 'too busy', which leaves the possibility that they were wiped out, as you say, yet the Confed Third Fleet is confirmed to have been lured elsewhere. Am I correct?"

"Yes, Sir. Desotoan Intelligence did indeed confirm the presence of the Confed fleet in the Bishti Sector."

"Could there be another Confed fleet here then? One that we are unaware of, perhaps?"

"I don't see how, Admiral. All that was left behind was a couple of squadrons of fighters and, of course, the Achaean Fleet."

"Such as it is."

"Yes, Sir. Such as it is."

Admiral de Ulloa nodded in sudden decision.

"Message to all Tenth Fleet commanders. Proceed toward Achaea at half speed. Destroyers out ahead as scouts. Let's find out what the hell happened here." He was silent for a moment as his orders were passed along. Then, he went on. "And we will destroy anyone who gets in our way!"

* * * *

Richard didn't have as deft a touch with an aircar as Kat. On the other hand, he didn't approach every landing as a combat assault into a hot LZ, either. So he alighted capably, if a bit awkwardly, in the car park near the Forerunner ruins.

He immediately exited the vehicle and followed the pathway toward the ruins. Richard noted idly that some security had been added since he'd been here last. Several uniformed guards were in evidence as he made his way to the pavilion where the archaeologists worked.

One of the guards stopped him short of the pavilion. "May I ask your business here, sir?"

The guard was polite enough, but Richard noticed that his hand hovered near a shock stick in his belt. The guard had no way of knowing that Richard could kill him before he got the stick unlimbered, and Richard didn't want to disillusion him. It never hurt to be polite. And if push came to shove, you could always kill or disable the guy later, if need be.

He gave the guard an innocent smile and said, "I'm here to see Doctor Brummett. We were out here last week when those unpleasant gentlemen tried to shoot the place up. I just wanted to ask the doctor some questions I didn't have a chance to ask because of the attack."

He could see things clicking behind the guard's eyes. Then, he smiled and said, "I was told that a man in a black robe took those scumbags out. Was that you, sir?"

Richard smiled modestly. "Guilty as charged, I'm afraid."

The other man nodded, smiling.

"In that case, I'm pretty sure the doctor will want to see you." He turned around and pointed toward the cliff face where the plasma rifle had blown a hole in the wall of some sort of chamber during the attack. "Doctor Brummett is right over there. They've been opening up that hole so that they can remove some of the larger artifacts, I guess."

Richard nodded and smiled again. "Thanks."

The robed Hawke headed toward the group working around the hole in the cliff face. He saw Professor Brummett directing the removal of small items. Each artifact was behind carefully photographed and wrapped in protective coatings before being placed in a container. One of the assistants was keeping a running inventory on a small tablet. Richard could see the holo of the inventory sheet, with small pictures of each item floating above the assistant's hands.

Richard really didn't know why, but he felt compelled to enter the cliff aperture. When one of the archaeologists asked him what he was doing, he ignored the man. The scientist put a hand on Richard's arm, and the man was suddenly airborne. Richard didn't even miss a stride.

As he came to the actual blast hole, the one-time monk could see that the opening had been widened to allow better access to the chamber beyond. Professor Brummett turned and saw Hawke heading toward the portal. He said, "Sir, you cannot enter this place. There are very ancient and sensitive artifacts in there!"

Richard glanced at him. "I know. I think that's why I'm here."

Another assistant tried to stop him. Richard

continued forward as this assistant too became airborne to land with a thud.

The black-robed man stepped up some wooden stairs into the chamber. A few artificial lights were arrayed around the walls, so that the scientists could see what they were doing. There were several large objects that were so alien in construction that Richard couldn't even guess at their function, or even if they had a function. Straight ahead there was a large, ovoid object with what looked like a very large chair in front of it.

Richard moved forward instinctively and first sat down, and then reclined in the "chair." Immediately, the ovoid began to glow. Then, all the large, oddly shaped objects around the ovoid began to glow as well. The brilliance intensified, getting brighter and brighter, until it was almost blinding.

Unbeknownst to Richard, Professor Brummett held up a staying hand as the security guard and some of his assistants moved to stop whatever Richard was doing. Brummett said, "Let him be. He's awakened something in the artifacts. Something powerful. I have to see what that something is!"

Richard gazed up at the rock ceiling, and it suddenly seemed to become transparent. No, more than transparent. He could see the stars and the planets of the Achaean system. And he could see ships and men moving across the firmament. It was as though he could just reach out and touch them. Richard reached out.

# Chapter 26: The Mountains

Jason ducked down among the rocks they were sheltering behind and gave a tight grin.

"I think these gentlemen have twigged to the fact that their pickets are disappearing." He hooked his head back in the direction he'd been scanning with his binocs. "There's a pretty large patrol heading this way in two vehicles, and they're armed to the teeth."

Ciera returned his smile.

"So we don't have to go hunting them. How convenient." Her smile turned into a fierce grin. "And we get to kill more Hashishiyun. This is a good thing!"

Roland looked at his brother. "I think she holds a bit of a grudge there, Bro."

Jason chuckled.

"Almost like a Hawke, don't you think?" He looked at the two of them. "Okay, how do you want to handle this?" Then he smiled broadly. "Oh wait, I've got an idea. Roland, how about all those claymores you packed along?"

Roland smiled just as broadly. "Oh yeah. I like the way you think, big brother. And you brought along that little rocket launcher you seemed so fond of, too."

Jason added, "And there's all that plastic explosive. Whatever shall we do with that?"

Ciera looked puzzled. "Claymores?"

* * * *

Hazim Al Assad was a member of one of the oldest families of the Hashisiyun on Alamut, and he was eager to prove himself to his commanders and his family. They had received reports of pickets being taken out. The consensus was that this was the work of a lone group of rebels. Hazim, and just about everyone else in his unit, had assumed that all such dissident bands had been purged long ago, but it appeared that this was not so. And it was now the job of the scion of the Al Assad family and twenty Assassins to make sure it was so again.

Fortunately, Hazim knew that the dissident movements on Alamut had been so decimated and weakened, that it had been years since the last round of executions. And any new rebels would have no access to modern weapons. The Hashishiyun had seen to that.

He was wrong on both counts. He found this out when the first explosion in the road overturned the troop carrier in front of him. Hazim's carrier had to swerve around the smoking wreckage, but when they did, they hit another mine.

Hazim assumed it had been a mine, of course, but it had actually been two packets of high explosive detonated by Roland Hawke from where he sat in the rocks above the road.

About half the troops were injured or dead, but Hazim, once he cleared his head, saw that he still had about fifteen effectives. The man next to him dropped when his head exploded. Make that fourteen effectives.

The remaining Assassins took cover behind the vehicles. None of them had been extensively trained in defensive fighting. It had always been assumed that they would be on the offensive, striking from the dark, always being unexpected and deadly.

Another man poked his head above the vehicle he sheltered behind. The man called, "They are in the rocks above us!"

He pointed to where he'd seen a muzzle flash. Then another gun flashed, and the man began dancing in an uncoordinated manner. Then, he dropped to the ground, dead.

* * * *

"Like a chicken with its head cut off," muttered Jason Hawke, "It happens that way sometimes."

"Nice shot," said his brother, Roland, "I can't believe you made it with that old smoke pole though."

Jason chuckled. "I like to use the old Mark One Calibrated Eyeball. Any technology can fail."

Roland patted his carbine. "But this particular tech has been around for a long time. Maybe not as long as that relic you're using, I grant you."

Roland raised up slightly and sighted in on the other truck. Sure enough, he got movement. He pressed a button on the sided of the rifle and pulled the trigger. The smart bullet struck the man he'd selected between the eyes. This one dropped straight down.

"Another blow for high tech!" Roland said, laughing.

Ciera Sultana gave them a grim smile, which looked odd on the face of such a pretty girl.

"Whatever method you use, a dead Assassin is a good Assassin to me." She gave the brothers a look of some admiration. "You are both quite good at this."

Jason was looking over the rocks. He glanced sidelong at the Alamut rebel. "A lifetime of practice will do that."

Jason stuck a periscope over the rocks. He watched for a moment, then he said, "I do believe they're about to try a frontal assault."

Roland looked over. "Up the trail to the right?"

"Well, that is the easiest way, but I think they have some brilliant strategist down there, and he's going to try to attack up both the left and right trails."

There was a savage yell from below as the Hashishiyun charged up the trails in question. It was clearly their intention to overwhelm their attackers with numbers and ferocity. They were halfway up the hill when the first claymores went off.

The claymore mine was invented way back in the twentieth century, and apart from advances in explosives and projectile alloys, had remained largely unchanged. The device basically consisted of a shaped charge of plastic explosive behind a bunch of round shot, rather like a large shotgun. Instead of eight or ten buckshot like a shotgun shell carried, however, the claymore had hundreds of such shot pellets. As a result, when the claymores along the two trails went off, they literally shredded the Assassins within their blast vector.

Hazim Al Assad was one of those so shredded. He'd felt that the honor of his family demanded that he lead the charge. The last things he heard were the shots that finished off the balance of his troop. The screaming ended somewhat after Hazim lost consciousness for the last time.

* * * *

Ciera Sultana looked around at the mangled and dismembered bodies with a cold stare. Then she looked up at Jason and asked, "What exactly is your strategy here? I mean, you're killing more Hashishiyun than anyone has ever succeeded in doing, but where are you going with this?"

Jason smiled and said, "Well, you could think of this as a reconnaissance by fire. By attacking, we flush out more of these thugs, and by killing them, still more will come after us."

"And then?"

Roland gave a short laugh. "And then we kill them. At some point, the Old Man will run out of Assassins."

Ciera gave him a fierce grin. "That would be good thing for my people. But once there are no more Assassins, what then?"

Jason gave her a grin that a hunting dire wolf would have envied. "Why then we kill the Old Man on the Mountain."

* * * *

By the next morning, the three were in a perch on a mountain crag overlooking a green valley. In the middle of the valley there was what looked like a prosperous town. And in the center of the town was a Citadel.

Ciera pointed at the Citadel. "There is the bastion of our enemy. That is the castle of Hassan i Sabbah, the Old Man on the Mountain. The Hashishiyun call it the Citadel of the Master."

# Chapter 27: Town of Assassins

Jason Hawke looked down from a crag in the mountains. Below him, in a beautiful mountain valley, was the Citadel of the Master. The fortification looked pretty old, right out of someone's medieval fantasy, but still most likely a tough nut to crack. After all, the three of them, although they did compose a crack spec ops team, were not designed for heavy assault. Taking those walls would probably require an armored unit, complete with a 20 cm plasma cannon. What they actually had were some smart weapons and, hopefully, some smart special ops people. So, how to use their strengths, and not play to the enemies' own strengths? Hmmm.

Between the Hawkes' party and the Citadel was a fair-sized town. But the town looked mostly empty, and, as he watched, a steady stream of the occupants of that town streamed into and through the gates of the Citadel.

Roland was also watching the evacuation. “Guess they heard we were coming.”

Ciera laughed.

“Such is not surprising, considering that we have destroyed five heavy patrols and about one hundred Hashishiyun. Such an assault has never been known in the history of Alamut. Those scum,” she hooked her chin at the Citadel, “don’t know how to handle you.” She gave a thoroughly nasty smile. “They are terrified.”

Jason was thoughtful. “I notice that most of the houses down there are quite large, some could reasonably be described as mansions. Ciera, can I safely assume that those places belong to the elite, the upper crust of the Hashishiyun?”

Sultana nodded. “Yes, they have grown bloated by leeching the wealth of the rest of the planet. Scum!”

She spit to emphasize her point.

Roland nodded at the rebel and told his brother, “She doesn’t like them much.”

“You think?” replied Jason, who seemed to somewhat preoccupied. “Miz Sultana, can I assume that the Assassins have families and that they would be living in the town?”

“Yes, of course.”

Jason looked grim. “Kids.”

He flashed back to Taegu. He and his commando team had hit a Tag prison camp. The last holdout building had been reduced using grenade launchers, and when Jason entered the smoking hulk of the building, the bodies of several children had been found. Apparently, some of the prison guards had brought along their families, and those dependents had taken shelter in that last redoubt when the Marines hit the camp.

Jason had taken it hard. He'd left the service and crawled down the neck of a bottle. It had been a long and painful road coming back from that, and only the fact that Kristin had been taken hostage by some Bishtian pirates had given him the heart to return from the brink. He would not willingly subject himself to that again.

Roland was gazing at the road to the Citadel. "I don't see any kids going into the Citadel. My guess is that they've already been evacuated."

Ciera added, "The children would have been sent away when they heard of our coming. My guess is that they were transported to a nearby city or even off planet. Those who are left are all Hashishiyun, many of their highest-level Families."

Roland chuckled. "Well, there are families, and then there are Families. The Hawke Family has now arrived."

Jason looked over at his two companions. "Does it seem odd that professional assassins could run scared like this? It seems totally out of character."

Ciera gave a grim chuckle. "Like I said, they have not had any significant opponents in many years. When anyone, like my father, spoke out against them, the whole family was murdered. It has been some time since anyone else has dared."

Jason looked back at the town.

"Well, if they're so shy about meeting us, we need to come up with some way of enticing them." He gestured at the town. "Those places look like mansions, and I would imagine that they contain much of value. If they were burnt, one by one, I suspect even these reluctant warriors might come out to protest."

"And when they do," Roland said, "we kill them."

"Exactly."

Ciera Sultana had a fierce look in her eyes. "Excellent!"

"Good," said Jason, "but first, I think we should slant things in our favor a bit."

* * * *

Jason, Roland, and Ciera split up and crept through the streets of the town. As unlikely as it had seemed, the place was really deserted. Nevertheless, they took care, staying in cover and concealment whenever possible and moving across open areas only when necessary. By two hours after dawn, they met at the end of the richer section of the town which was farthest from the Citadel.

Jason looked at his two companions. "Are all the traps set?"

Ciera nodded. "Yes. I used all the explosives and mini-mines you gave me, and I also improvised some traps of my own."

Roland chuckled. “Ah, the ubiquitous IEDs! I, too, set some of those. They can be quite useful.”

Jason smiled. “And deadly, knowing you two. Okay, I think it’s time to start blowing shit up.”

He took a small detonator from his tactical vest and keyed a code. Instantly, flame poured into the morning sky from two huge mansions. The flames and debris reached into the sky, impossible to miss.

“And again,” he said.

Three more huge houses disappeared in smoke and flames.

Jason gave a grim smile. “Okey dokey. Now we wait. If nobody pokes their heads out of the Citadel, we blow a few more mansions. At some point, they’ll either run out of houses in this town or come out to engage us.”

Three house fires later, Roland called, “I’ve got movement on the left and right of the Citadel. I make ten bogies in each group. Looks like they’re armed to the teeth.”

Jason nodded.

“Cool. Roland, you and Ciera take the group to our left. I’ll take the ones to our right.” He smiled. “Twenty to one odds. Against Hawkes, I figure we have them outnumbered.”

With that, Jason ghosted off toward the group he’d indicated. Keeping to shadows where possible, he carried his rifle at the ready. They’d seen no one in the town at all, but he still had the discipline to not want to shoot noncombatants. At the same time, he was very ready to shoot Hashishiyun. He'd already been angry at them after the attempted assassination of the Moderator, but now that he'd seen how they treated their own people, well, it certainly appeared that the universe could do quite well without them, and their Old Man, too.

While setting their booby traps and waiting for the inevitable strike forces from the Citadel, Jason and his team had picked out likely perches for snipers. This served two purposes. First, it made them aware of places they might take fire from, and, second, it gave them a good idea where they could deliver accurate fire on the enemy. In urban combat, it was unlikely, but not impossible, that any targets would be more than three hundred meters away.

In the next block, therefore, Jason entered a four-story building (There were no real skyscrapers in the town of the Hashishiyun.) and quickly climbed the stairs to the roof. There, he set up his scoped rifle and, using mini-binocs, surveyed the streets between him and the Citadel. In fairly short order, he saw movement. The bad guys were on the way to their destiny.

Next, he surveyed nearby high buildings, and sure enough, there was an enemy sniper. Jason continued his survey, but there was only the one sniper on a perch. No doubt he was there to provide counter-sniper fire.

Moving as little as possible, Jason quickly checked the location of the rest of the party. Good. They were coming into range of some of his mini-claymores.

"This should give them something to think about," he muttered. Touching one button on a com pad next to him, he set off the first mines.

There was a blast, and several of the ground troops dropped. The rest of them took cover where they could, which was kind of haphazard, since they didn't really know where the ambusher was.

Jason re-settled his rifle into his shoulder and acquired the roof where the other sniper was. And he was indeed still there. In fact, he was leaning over the edge of the roof to see what had happened.

"Dumbfuck." Jason exhaled slowly and squeezed the trigger. The Hashishiyun sniper fell all the way over the parapet to the street below.

"Now for his buddies."

Jason took aim on the street where a leg was visible around the side of a building. The rifle kicked again, and there was a splash of red.

* * * *

Roland and Ciera heard the shots from the other side of the town, but they were otherwise occupied. The group of Hashishiyun approaching them was coming into range of their weapons, which was about one hundred meters closer than the range of Jason's dedicated sniper rifle.

Because of that differential, Roland had decided to meet their enemies at ground level, which made life more interesting, anyway.

Although they were still out of sight, Roland could tell when the Assassins' point man found the trip wire for the first IED, because there was a sudden explosion and multiple screams.

Ciera smiled. "Ah, they do not like it so well when the shoe is on the other foot!"

Then a second group of five Hashishiyun charged them from around a building to their left. Roland dropped one of them with his carbine before the remaining Assassins were upon them. He used the carbine as a short staff, butt stroking the man on his right to the temple. That put that one out of the fight, either temporarily or permanently.

Roland ducked as the other Hashishiyun slashed the air where his head had been with a scimitar. He realized that this opponent was a woman, and a woman with very fast reflexes. Hawke blocked another overhead slash with his carbine, dropped back into a reverse bo stance, and met the woman's charge with a rear kick that lifted her off the ground and launched her through the air to impact one of the two Assassins engaged with Ciera. The two went down in a tangle of limbs.

Free to concentrate on only one opponent, a man twice her size wielding another of those scimitars, Ciera dropped to the ground and broke the man's left knee with a kick. The Hashishiyun screamed and dropped to the ground, landing on the other two killers.

Picking up the sword the woman attacker had dropped, Roland raised it above his head, and with two hands on the hilt, drove the blade through all three bodies.

Ciera looked at him, wide-eyed.

Roland flashed her a fighting grin and said, "That should hold them for a while. Time to change position."

There would be more enemies to kill.

## Chapter 28: Castille

Cuchulain Hawke and Gemma Jackson made their exit out of the Cortez Tower through the front doors. No alarms were activated, and no guards tried to stop them. Once they exited the main doors and crossed the street, Gemma spoke a code word into a small controller disguised as a charm on her bracelet. A huge explosion smashed outwards from the 190th to the 200th floors.

Galaxy Imports had ceased to exist.

Koo looked over at her with some admiration. “So that’s what you were doing when you were caught?”

She gave him a tight smile. “Yeah. Thank goodness they caught me after I’d set the explosives! As it was, they were only suspicious that I was up to no good, for them at least.”

He nodded. “But if they’d seen the charges, they would have known for sure, and they might have been even less polite.”

“Polite!” she snorted.

“Well, polite for Desotoan agents, anyway. You’re not missing any limbs, and you don’t have any broken bones. Of course, I suspect they were just getting warmed up when I dropped by.”

She gave him a hard smile. “Yes, you just dropped by. By the way, thank you.”

He gave her a short bow. “No problem. Happy to be of service.”

She gave him a sharp look. “So how is it that you just ‘dropped by’ in the middle of a high-security enclosure on the 195th floor of a building on one of the core planets of the Desotoan Empire? Are you a Desotoan agent?”

He noticed a dangerous light in her eyes that turned to one of astonishment when he laughed.

“Me? A Desotoan agent?” He began laughing again.

Gemma couldn’t help but smile at his genuine laughter. “So why were you there? And how did you get into the offices?”

At this point, Koo decided it would be silly to try to claim that he was an innocent civilian, and Gemma was clearly an agent who really didn’t like the Desotoans. Worst case, they had a common enemy.

"My name is Cuchulain Hawke. Some weeks ago, an agent tried to recruit my family to assassinate some unnamed persons. At this point, I would guess that at least one of those persons was the Moderator. My Dad turned this guy down, and the gentleman in question then tried to kill my Dad, my Mom, and me. My family took exception to these actions. The Hawkes really don't put up with shit like that. And Dad sent me to find out who was behind the attempt. At this point, it seems most likely it was Desotoan Intelligence." He gave her a stern look. "And here you killed off the entire office of those scumbags. My father is going to be very unhappy with you."

Gemma walked along, clearly deep in thought. Then, her eyes widened, and she came to a sudden stop. She looked Koo right in the eyes and said, "Wait a minute. Your name is Hawke? As in the Hawke Clan? The greatest assassins in the galaxy?"

He nodded modestly. "That would be us. I'm impressed though. Not all that many people have heard of the family. I suspect that your parents aren't the 'minor bureaucrats' you said they were, either."

She turned and started walking again. She also had the grace to look a bit embarrassed. "Well, yeah. My parents were both Confed field agents back in the day. My Dad is sector chief for the CI Nihon office."

Cuchulain did not find any of this surprising at this point. "So you're in the family business, just like I am."

She gave him a faint smile. “I guess. But our business is working for the Confederation. Your family are hired assassins!”

“You say that like it’s a bad thing. Actually, we’ve done quite a bit of work for the Confed over the years. And we are very careful about what jobs we do take. Witness this most recent fracas. The whole thing smelled fishy to my Dad, so we refused to take the job.”

They walked in silence for a few minutes, wanting to put distance between themselves and any exploding buildings.

Then Gemma said, “Well, I need to contact with the local office and let them know about the confirmed Desotoan involvement in the attempted assassination.”

Koo nodded. “And I need to call home as well. My father is not going to be amused in either the fact that the Desotoans were involved, or that they tried to get us to kill the Moderator.”

“But what can he do?”

“He’ll probably want to register a complaint.”

Gemma was puzzled. “But who would he complain to? And why would anyone listen? He’s only one man.”

Cuchulain laughed so loudly that several passers by smiled to see the handsome couple having such a good time.

He said, “Temujin Hawke, only one man? True enough, I guess. But I’m pretty sure he’s going to register his complaint anyway. And he’ll take his complaint right to the top.”

“The top of what?”

“The top of the Desotoan Empire. Like I said, he’s going to be really pissed. And you have no idea what it means to get my Dad angry.”

# Chapter 29: Achaea

The Confederation ASPs and Vipers sortied out from Achaea, making for the incoming Desotoan fleet. There were only ten of the Viper fighters left, minus the one Kat had crashed into an office building and another destroyed by enemy fire during the previous mission. Actually, in the kind of action they'd been involved in, only losing two fighters had been very good luck. This time, though, the odds were steeper, and their luck might not be so good.

Nor would they receive as much support from the Achaean Navy. The locals were sending out their cruiser and one destroyer, but even their surviving ships had sustained significant damage from the other Desotoan task force, and neither was up to one hundred percent.

For that matter, although they had acquitted themselves well, the Achaean ships hadn't gotten any newer, and according to the Achaean scouts, the incoming threat was even larger, with more capital ships. The last task force had only had two cruisers. According to the reports, this one had four cruisers and two battleships.

It was with a flash of respect that Kat saw the two Achaean ships closing on her monitors. She had to admit, those guys had big brass ones. Their admiral might be a bit of a blowhard, but there wasn't any back-down in him.

But all of the courage in the world couldn't change these odds. As it was, the two Achaean ships were approaching the enemy fleet in the ecliptic, with the Confed fighters coming in from above. The ASPs were coming in from below. Both of the Confed contingents were completely stealthed. Kat figured they'd be able to bloody the Desotoans' noses, but after that, things were going to get messy.

At extreme range, the Desotoans began firing missiles.

* * * *

Admiral de Ulloa saw the pitiful number of icons on the tactical screen on his flag bridge, and snorted in contempt. "They are pathetic! What do they hope to accomplish with so few ships?"

Captain Manuel Coronado, de Ulloa's flag captain and commander of the battleship, DSS Franco, was in open contact with the admiral. "Admiral, if they indeed wiped out our earlier task force, perhaps they have become overconfident."

The admiral gave a short bark of laughter. "Well, if so, we are about to disabuse them of such confidence. Open fire!"

Coronado was careful to not sound too incredulous. "But sir, we are outside the optimum envelope for our ship-killing missiles."

Ulloa gave the flag captain a look that promised future retribution. "Perhaps, but it will give these fools something to think about. And if they have some sort of trap laid, which I very much doubt, this should cause them to spring it early."

This logic was so specious, that Coronado had to take a deep breath before he said something irretrievably caustic. Instead, he replied, "Aye-aye, Admiral."

To his tactical officer, the flag captain said, "TACO, order all units to open fire."

"Aye-aye, Sir!"

* * * *

Lieutenant Commander James Lewis saw the icons for missile launches from the Desotoan ships. There were an awful lot of them, but what the heck were they doing firing from so far away? "Chief, what the hell do they think they're going to accomplish by firing when they're still out of effective range?"

Chief Petty Officer Jim Wilson chuckled. "Who knows, Sir. They're Desotoans, after all. If I had to guess, they're either trying to scare the Achaeans, or they're trying to flush out an ambush."

Lewis watched the missile tracks, all of which were aimed in the general direction of the Achaean Navy ships, all two of them. "You're probably right, Chief, but it offends my sense of professionalism. And for that matter, if they're really trying to flush out an ambush, they missed their mark. They don't seem to have picked up either our boats or the Vipers. I mean, I know we're fully stealthed and on a ballistic course, but jeeze!"

"And that is totally okay by me, Boss. We may just get a piece of those bastards after all."

"Well, if we just get a little closer, I'm going to rain on their parade."

* * * *

Lieutenant Colonel Gareth Blaustein had the same reaction to the early launch. He didn't want to break comm silence, since that would pretty much negate the whole point of being in full stealth mode, but he knew that his squadron was seeing the same thing he was seeing on their passive sensors.

Just a little closer.

* * * *

The Achaean ships weathered the storm of missiles that came their way from the Desotoans for precious seconds. The Greeks were armed with Confed ship-killers, and the Confederation missiles had significantly greater range than the Desotoan versions.

High Admiral Lysandros Maimonides watched the displays on his flag bridge. The range was closing. Closing.

The admiral commed the captains of his two ship fleet. "Fire as you bear!"

Ship-killing missiles shot out from the Achaean ships toward the incoming enemy fleet.

* * * *

Captain Coronado commed Admiral de Ulloa. "Admiral, the Achaeans have launched missiles."

Ulloa snorted. "So what? They were bound to try. Not that they can accomplish anything significant."

Coronado nodded.

"Yes, Sir." Then, his attention jerked away from the display. In a much more alarmed voice, he said, "Admiral, we're getting multiple missile launches from both above and below the ecliptic!"

Ulloa still wasn't impressed. "OK. We figured they must have some sort of ambush set up. Deal with it. Clear."

Coronado was speaking to a dead com link when he said, "But we're seeing hundreds of launches, Sir, and they're all aimed at our battleships."

The flag captain realized that Ulloa wasn't listening anymore, and said to his bridge crew. "Launch countermissiles, and find those missile platforms and kill them!"

* * * *

Kat could tell that the Desotoan warships had picked up the missiles the fighters and ASPs had launched at them, but both had gone right back into stealth mode after the initial launch. Now the range was closing, and soon the active sensors of the Desotoans would pick them up even if they were stealthed. And then the battle would really begin, although it promised to be a very short battle for the Confed forces. There were just too many of the enemy ships, and the Achaeans and the Confeds were fighting way out of their weight class.

For a moment, she wondered why she'd volunteered to join this fight, but deep down she knew she couldn't have sat on the sidelines and let the people of the Confed squadrons, many of whom had become her friends, go it alone. She thought of Richard, and was glad that he was out of harm's way.

* * * *

In a cave on the surface of the planet Achaea, Richard Hawke was in a trance. At least, that was how it appeared to the archaeologists who stood near the entrance of the Forerunner store house.

A blue glow had sprung up to enclose Hawke and the "chair" he reclined on. Apparently, the blue glow was, at least in part, a force field. And when a security guard tried to approach Richard, the guard was kicked back ten meters to slam into one of the walls of the cavern.

But although Richard appeared to be in a trance, his mind was racing. Somehow, the Forerunner equipment, for that was what the relics were, was operational, and it was attuned to a mind very like Richard Hawke's. A mind accustomed to meditation and exploring the inner reaches of the human mind and spirit.

And Richard's mind soared. He seemed to be suspended in space, the space of the Achaean system. He could sense every planet, every asteroid, and the ships of the two opposing forces. In this state, all the strivings of the warships and their occupants seemed meaningless, mundane. Richard could hear the music of the heavens, and the sound was sweet.

But then he perceived one mind in all those thousands of minds striving in the reaches of space. One mind that thought of him; that had a bond to him. And he knew that it was Kat Dunvegan, and she expected to die.

He felt her love for him, and his corresponding love for her, and he knew that he could not let her die, even if it meant his own death.

Richard looked more closely at the ships, and he could see the difference between the Desotoan capital ships and the ragtag force opposing them. He could also see forces and patterns in the space around them.

Richard Hawke reached out with his mind, grasped those forces somehow, and twisted.

Massive battleships with thousands of crewmembers, and huge battlecruisers with hundreds more were caught in those forces, and they just ceased to exist.

The strain was too much for a mere human, though, and Richard Hawke was swallowed in a black maw.

* * * *

Lieutenant Commander James Lewis gaped at the sensor screens and said, “What the hell just happened?”

Chief Petty Officer Jim Wilson shook his head. “Damned if I know, Sir.” He looked at the empty space where the huge Desotoan warships had been. “But, one thing I do see. Those Desotoan destroyers are uncovered, Boss.”

Lewis managed to re-focus with an effort. “You’re absolutely right, Chief. Let’s kill them.” He got on the ship to ship comm, and shouted, “All ASPs, attack the destroyers!”

The Desotoans were still in shock when the Confed missiles from the ASPS and Vipers came hurtling at them. Their shock lasted just moments too long. Multiple missile hits started smashing into the Desotoans, and they turned and ran.

# Chapter 30: Citadel

Roland rolled over from where he'd been surveying the town of the Hashishiyun through mini-binocs. He looked over at Jason and Ciera. "I haven't seen any movement in over an hour. How many of these assholes did we kill here in the town?"

Jason replied, "I make it as about fifty here and more like a hundred on the way." He looked over at Ciera. "How many active fighters do these guys have, anyway?"

She shook her head.

"No one has ever seen more than ten at a time. They usually operate in two or three man teams. They don't need a whole lot of actives, because they never fight fixed-place engagements. They are always the aggressors, and they pick the time and place." She looked over at the Citadel and said, "Until now." She turned back to the Hawke brothers. "I believe they are scared now."

The girl whose family had been killed by the Hashishiyun gave a smile that a hunting sabertooth would have been proud of. "I like that."

Jason gave her a toothy smile of his own, and then turned back to the Citadel. "Well, they should be scared. But now comes the hard part. We need to get into their Citadel, and we need to kill the Old Man."

Roland said, in a very dry tone, "I do believe that the remaining Hashishiyun might object."

"Good," his brother agreed, "I'm not too happy with them anyway."

* * * *

The three moved carefully, keeping to cover and concealment as much as possible, and crossing open areas quickly. Nobody tried to kill them. They stopped behind the corner of a building about one quarter mile from the open side gates.

Roland looked over at Jason. "Ambush?"

"Duh. Of course they're planning an ambush. But at least that way, we don't have to search for them."

"True."

The three moved carefully across the open area in front of the gate. No one tried to kill them, which Jason considered a plus.

The gates were a huge double-doored affair, more suitable for a medieval fantasy than for the modern worlds of high technology and space travel. Roland nodded at him and gestured towards the opening.

Jason became a blur of motion. There were basically two ways of entering a probably hostile environment: really fast, or slow and cautious. Jason had never been a fan of slow and cautious. It made you too much of a target for too long. Jason dove across the gateway toward the right side of the courtyard beyond.

No one shot at him, but about the time he came to his feet in a fighting crouch, three of the green-clad cyborg assassins came storming out of the large double doors on the opposite side of the courtyard.

"Necks!" he shouted.

He and Roland had found out the hard way that the Greenies' torsos and heads were pretty bulletproof.

Jason dropped his rifle and drew his wakizashi. Roland and Ciera showed themselves to get better shots. The muzzle of Roland's seeker carbine flashed twice, and the eyes of the nearest Greenie disappeared in a splash of gore.

Knowing that these guys generally relied on their brute strength and near-invlunerability, Jason did a quick sidestep and slashed his sword across the Hashishiyun's neck. The cyborg's rush continued, but his head suddenly dropped off to one side. In two more steps, the body joined the head.

The last Greenie charged directly at Ciera Sultana. She calmly raised her shotgun and shot at the juncture of the neck and head. The shot literally blew the Hashishiyun's head completely off.

Roland looked over at her handiwork. "Not elegant," he opined, "but that works too."

"Good to know," said Jason. "Let's keep moving."

Since the Greenies had come out of the main doors, it was reasonably certain the portal wasn't booby-trapped. Nevertheless, Roland threw a severed Greenie head through the doorway. When nothing exploded, he nodded to Jason.

Jason took point, and went in fast, using they technique they'd already used successfully coming in the gates. This time, there were no attackers, so they moved on. There were huge, curving staircases leading up to an upper floor and wide corridors to their left, right, and straight ahead.

Jason jerked his head to the stairs. "Like Dad always said, start at the top and work your way down." He started toward the right staircase.

At Ciera's questioning look, Roland explained, "That way, you don't miss anything, and you don't leave anybody in your rear."

She nodded. "Got it."

The three moved quietly up the stairs, with Ciera and Roland taking the left staircase. At the top, they found hallways leading both to the right and the left. With hand gestures, Jason indicated that he would take the right and they were to take the left corridor. Roland nodded and gestured to Ciera. They moved out.

Jason had his rifle slung. He was pleased, and a bit surprised, that it had not been damaged when he'd thrown it aside in the face of the first Greenie attack. Now, he moved silently with his short sword in his right hand and a high-velocity pellet pistol in his left. Temujin had taught them to be ambidextrous as well as to highly develop their situational awareness. That training was now coming useful, as it had all too often in the past.

There were rooms on both sides of the corridor, and Jason cleared each room as he went. In some cases, the doors were locked, but the wakizashi served as an excellent lock pick. Made in the form of the ancient Japanese short sword, the Hawkes' wakizashis were made of the same battle steel used in the hulls of Confederation warships. The metal of the locking mechanisms didn't stand a chance.

Just ahead of him, two of the green-clad Hashishiyun burst out of doors on opposite sides of the hallway. Raising the pistol, Jason put two pellets into the cyborg on the left; one in the throat and one in his left eye. Then he dropped the pistol and moved to meet the other Greenie. This one was bigger than any of the others he'd run into, and his favored technique seemed to be a brute force rush. This was not someone Jason wanted to get into a grappling fight with.

In the combat arts, it is all too easy to fall into a rut and focus only on techniques that have worked successfully in the past. In the case of the Hashishiyun, especially these Greenies, they never seemed to see the need to diversify. Temujin Hawke, on the other hand, had pounded into his sons the need to be expert at all forms of combat. Thus it was that although each of the brothers had a set of favored strategies and weapons, they were all not just conversant, but expert, in many different techniques and weapons systems.

The other thing that the brothers had noticed was that the cyborgs did not use weapons. This was very useful in assassination missions, and, indeed, the Hawkes had relied on that many times in the past. Guards looked for weapons, and if the assassin didn't carry any, said guards were lulled into a false sense of security. The cyborg's innards were also armored against most weapons that would be used on them, so they were in good shape both offensively and defensively.

But, any ideals of martial arts purity aside, the Hawke clan recognized that weapons were useful tools. For that matter, as Temujin had often said, the term "martial" was derived from Mars, the Roman god of war. Mars was not the god of unarmed combat.

Now, Jason Hawke introduced the cyborg bull to war. Dropping into a right bo stance, Jason sliced his blade across the eyes of the Hashishiyun. The cyborg's skull might be armored, but his eyes were not. The Greenie lurched to his own left, his hands going to his blood-streaming eye sockets. Jason popped back up to an upright posture, and taking a two-hand grip on his short sword, he sliced from right to left, neatly removing the cyborg's head. Both body and head dropped to the tiled floor.

Jason moved ahead down the corridor.

* * * *

The first straight part of the left corridor was empty, as were the rooms along it. Roland and Ciera checked each one, covering one another as they entered each apartment.

As they came around the corner of what was apparently a series of hallways that completely circumnavigated the Citadel, three green-clad Hashishiyun charged them.

Roland was on the right, so he shot the Greenie on the far right, double-tapping his eyes. The man screamed and dropped. He heard Ciera's shotgun go off to his left, but the middle cyborg, a woman this time, had launched herself at him with a flying side kick. Roland was slightly surprised, since flying kicks are pretty useless against a trained opponent. Once you're in the air, you're committed, and they telegraph from a mile away. On the other hand, since the cyborgs were armored just about everywhere except the neck and eyes, maybe it wasn't so stupid.

But against Roland Hawke, it was a fatal decision. He simply sidestepped, brought his pellet pistol up, and fired two times into the woman's throat as she flew by. Blood splashed across the room.

Roland figured the wounds were fatal, but the Hashishiyun's body hadn't figured that out yet, and she landed like a cat, knocking the pistol out of his hand with one metallized foot. The woman then tried to follow up with a high kick to Roland's head, but he trapped her foot, and, pivoting 180° he used the inertia of the force behind her kick to throw her in a parabolic arc, which ended abruptly when her head hit a door jamb. There was a sickening crunch, and her body finally decided it was dead.

Ciera attempted to duplicate her feat from the courtyard and fired her shotgun, hoping to blow off the head of her attacker. Unfortunately, the large male cyborg ducked his head, and all she accomplished was to jelly one of his eyes and blow his left ear off.

The Assassin was staggered from the shot, but then he resumed his charge. Ducking low, Ciera knocked one foot out from under the Greenie, who crashed to the floor. Ciera jumped up and landed with both feet on the back of the man's neck. The neck snapped, and the Hashishiyun was still. Forever.

Roland looked over at her. "Good job. Very creative."

She looked sick, but she managed a small smile. "You try to be an orphan and a girl on the streets of a city and planet run by the Hashishiyun. You learn fast, or you die."

Around the next corner, they met Jason. He said, "That's the upper floor. Let's go downstairs and start the real party."

# Chapter 31: The Center of Power

Jason, Roland, and Ciera Sultana made it back down the main floor unmolested. In this case, a huge portal opened into one large corridor. It looked like other similarly large hallways intersected it about fifty yards down, and at the very end was a set of huge golden doors with elaborate carvings even evident from this distance.

Jason looked at Roland and both nodded. Jason said, "Let's rock and roll."

They moved forward. Ciera carried her shotgun at high port. Each of the Hawke brothers carried a short sword in one hand and a pistol in the other. No sense changing techniques that worked.

Suddenly, the golden doors opened, more quickly than Jason would have expected, given their apparent weight, and ten more of the green-clad Hashishiyun charged out.

Roland said, calmly, “The good news is, none of them appears to be armed.”

Jason snorted. “Sure, they’re just bulletproof, super-strong, and super-fast.”

Ciera surprised herself by chuckling. “Always looking at the dark side, you two. There are more of them to kill.”

Then, they were engaged.

Ciera fired her shotgun twice, and at least one of those was fatal. Then, she was hurtling across the corridor, where she made an abrupt impact with the wall. Bouncing off, she tried to stand, only to find that her right knee wasn’t working properly. She could see the shotgun lying in the middle of the hallway, but the melee of fighting figures surging around it meant that there was no way she could crawl or hop to regain it. In what seemed a futile gesture of defiance, she drew a large fighting knife. At least she’d go down fighting!

Then she saw the bodies. At least five of the cyborgs were down. A couple had gaping holes where their eyes used to be; one’s head was twisted around so that he could have gotten a good look at his heels; and two were missing their heads entirely. The beautiful marble floor of the corridor was sticky with blood and stank of death.

As she watched, two more green-clad figures hit the ground. Well, one hit the wall, only to slide back down, his throat gushing blood. Then she saw the Hawkes. The Greenies were inhumanly fast, but the Hawkes were faster. The Hashishiyun were incredibly strong, but the Hawkes were even stronger. And the Hawkes' extremely advanced training was evident. Compared to them, the cyborgs seemed sluggish and clumsy. She realized that the brothers were anticipating every move, and were at least two steps ahead of the Assassins. In fact, she saw what the human form could be, and the semi-human cyborgs were no match for them.

In mere moments, the corridor was still. There was still some slight movement from two of the cyborgs, but is was muscle twitches from bodies that didn't realize they were dead yet.

In the center of the hallway, Jason and Roland Hawke stood, covered in blood, but it appeared that not much of it was theirs. There were rents and tears in their camouflage uniforms. One whole sleeve was ripped away from Jason's. But both brothers were conscious, alert, and still very deadly.

Around them were the bodies of ten green-clad cyborgs.

She looked at them in awe.

"But those were the greatest assassins in the galaxy!" She looked them searchingly. "What are you?"

Jason gave a grim laugh. "They only thought they were assassins. We are Hawkes. Our family are the greatest assassins ever."

He seemed to feel that explained it all, and maybe it did.

Roland came over and offered her a hand. “Come on, it’s time we paid a visit to the Old Man.”

Ciera noticed that both of the Hawke brothers were injured. They might be great assassins, certainly the greatest warriors she’d ever seen or heard of, but they weren’t invulnerable. Roland had tucked his right arm into his belt as a sort of makeshift sling, and he had bloody furrows across the left side of his face. Jason was limping a bit and favored his left side. It looked like some cracked ribs there, at least.

But both of them were still up and mobile, and their opponents were dead. If there were any more Hashishiyun fighters left, her money would be on the Hawkes.

Using her shotgun as a crutch, she joined Roland and Jason Hawke as they walked through the golden doors at the end of the hallway.

The next room was opulent in the extreme. Roland looked around and chuckled.

“Not much like home, is it Bro?” He looked over at Ciera. “Dad is pretty Spartan in home and furnishings, although after all the centuries the Hawkes have been in business, I know he must have a significant fortune socked away. But he didn’t believe in being overly comfortable or ostentatious. Dad always said he figured it would make us soft.” He gesture around him. “Now this would be the other end of the spectrum.”

Fine woods, gold-encrusted screens and panels, and objets d'art liberally festooned with precious stones adorned the large room. It looked like the throne room of some barbarian potentate.

"Ah," said Jason, "I believe that is our host."

He pointed to the opposite end of the room.

On a low dais before them, there was what could only be called a throne. It was just as ornate and just as overdone as the rest of the room, but it was hard to see it, for the occupant was fat. No, he wasn't just fat, he was grotesquely obese, his waistline overlapping the arms of the throne.

Roland chuckled. "I even think they ordered the extra-jumbo sized throne for him, but he outgrew it. He must be a good eight hundred pounds."

As they drew near, a high-pitched, whining voice came from the man on the throne. "What are you doing here? Guards! Guards!"

Ciera looked at the pathetic hunk of lard and said, "I don't think your guards are in any shape to come to your aid. We're looking for the Old Man on the Mountain, the head of the Hashishiyun. Where is he, you great sack of suet?"

"Shut up, bitch," the whiner snapped, "I am the Old Man, and my word is law on this world! You will all die horrible deaths for this insolence!"

The look in Ciera Sultana's eyes could have flayed the skin off a dinosaur. "So you would have us killed, just like you had my family killed?"

“Yes!” the Old Man cried, “You will all be killed!”

Ciera shook her head. “Not this time. This ends here.”

She drew her knife.

Jason looked over at Roland. “Let’s leave these two alone to sort out their differences.”

He and his brother strolled out toward the main corridor. Behind them, the screams began.

* * * *

They were back at their landing craft. They’d taken the time to clean up a bit in the town of the Assassins outside the Citadel of the Old Man, and then headed back to the ship.

Ciera smiled at them and said, “Won’t you stay for a while? I could use some help putting things back together here.”

Jason hugged her and said, “Naw. We’re done here, and besides, you don’t need our help.”

Roland hugged her in turn. He smiled and said, “Yeah, you’re the Old Man on the Mountain now.”

“I can’t do what those scum did.”

Jason nodded. “Then do something different. But don’t write off the whole Assassins thing. There’s always a need for surgical takeouts. Just don’t get too over-impressed with yourselves.”

Roland chuckled. “After all, if things get too bad, somebody might send us back.”

She gave a tight smile. “That will not be necessary. Good fortune, and good hunting!”

With that, she turned and headed back to her vehicle.

Roland turned back toward the lander. “Come on, Bro. Let’s get the hell off this dirtball!”

# Chapter 32: Powers Behind the Throne

Cuchulain Hawke and Gemma Jackson had just lifted off from the Desotoan planet of Cadiz. They hadn't filed a course with Cadiz Ground Control. In fact, they hadn't let Ground Control know they were leaving at all. That had something to do with the fact that they were aboard a stolen yacht some careless grandee had left unattended.

The increasingly threatening hails from first Cadiz Ground Control and then the system gendarmerie in their patrol cutters had finally ended. That didn't mean they were any less irate. It just mean that Koo had shut off the comm unit.

He said, "You know, I'm totally impressed that you know how to drive one of these things." He looked at the dead comm unit. "And I don't think they like us anymore down there."

"Well, first of all, thank you. Piloting a starship is part of my Central Intelligence training. And I agree," Gemma replied, "let's not include Cadiz on our next itinerary. What do you think?"

Koo grinned. "Sounds good to me. Speaking of which, we probably need to decide where we do want to go from here."

She nodded. "Good point. To that end, see if you can get the FTL link on this bucket up and running. Since there were all those gendarmes around the CI office on Cadiz, I still have to contact my superiors. Once I send them the data packet I retrieved from Galactic, they'll decide where they want to send me next."

"Good thinking. I also need to contact home base. Well, I need to get a hold of my Dad and see what he wants me to do next." He looked long-suffering. "He'll probably yell at me for something."

* * * *

"Dad, this is Koo. We just bid a fond farewell to that vacation spot, the planet of Cadiz. The source of the attempted hit on us was one Enrique Balboa, head of Desotoan Security."

"Good," his father replied, "Your mission is now concluded."

"Are you sure? You don't want me to take out this Balboa dude?"

"No, I'm sure you will have become too visible by this time. I'll take care of Balboa, and in such a way that this won't happen again."

"But..."

"Koo, you've done a fine job. Leave the rest to me."

"Yes, Sir."

He looked at Gemma wonderingly.

"He said I did a fine job. And he didn't yell at me." He paused. "That's a first."

She smiled. "Well, you saved my life. I figure that comes under the heading of a 'fine job.' My turn."

* * * *

Gemma looked over at Cuchulain once she'd finished comming her superiors. "I guess I'm off the case. They said they had all the info they needed. I can head home."

Koo nodded.

"Me too. Let's set course for the Confederation." He looked thoughtful. "You know, it's going to take us a week to get back to Starcastle. Whatever shall we do in the meantime?"

She gave him a grin. "Oh, I'm sure we'll think of something!"

* * * *

When Richard awoke, he was back in the hospital in Mycenae. He recognized the pattern of dots on the ceiling. "I need to quit doing this."

A voice answered. “I agree.”

Kat came into his view. She was smiling.

“You’ve been in a coma for three days, you big lunk!” She bent over and hugged him fiercely. “What the heck happened to you? When I left, you were just fine.”

A memory stirred.

“I went out to the Forerunner ruins. After that, it gets kind of blurry.” He looked over at her. “You seem in good health. Did we win?”

She nodded. “Absolutely. It was so weird. Both sides had launched ship-killers, and some hits were made. Then, it looked like the Desotoan heavies were about to put a big boot down on us, and they just vanished! Like, poof!”

He smiled.

“Poof?” Then his brow furrowed. “I remember when I was in the ruins. They’d found some ancient Forerunner equipment that looked completely intact. I sat down on one of the pieces of equipment. It was like a big chair, then I started seeing things. It was like I could see the whole solar system, and beyond. I saw the ships of the two fleets. And I saw you.”

He gave her a wondering look. “I could see you, sense you, and I could see those other ships that were going to hurt you. And I made them go away.”

Her eyebrows rose.

“You made them go away? Just like that?” She snapped her fingers.

“Pretty much,” he replied, “After that, I woke up here.”

She thought for a long moment.

"I suggest we neglect to mention that thing about the fleet if anybody asks." She hugged him again. "Otherwise, we might never get you out of here."

He hugged her back. "Agreed. Let's get me out of here as soon as possible."

* * * *

Gwendolyn landed at the executive terminal at Starcastle Spaceport. Scottie came back to the berths where Jason and Roland were getting ready to debark. He said, "I got a call. CI wants to debrief you as soon as possible."

Jason snorted. "Not going to happen. If anybody is going to de-brief me, it's going to be my wife."

Roland laughed. "Yeah, screw Central Intelligence. They'll get their report when I'm done composing it. In the meantime, I have a hot date with a beautiful brunette."

Scottie held up his hands.

"Hey, I'm just passing the message along. As it happens, I do believe there's a bottle of rum with my name on it at my favorite Starcastle bar." He gave them a short wave. "See you guys. Have fun. And don't forget my bonus!"

Jason said, "Thanks, Scottie. I plan on having rather a lot of fun. And no, I won't forget your bonus!"

Roland added. "Yeah, let's get out of this tub. I have been aboard ship and staring at your ugly mugs for way too long."

Jason hugged him. "Thanks, Bro. I'll see you in a couple of days. I'll tell Kristin you said Hi."

"Cool."

As it happened, both Kristin Baird and Gillian Straley were waiting for them in the terminal.

Gillian walked up to Roland. "Nice job. Promotions in the works and all that. And now that the business part of our meeting is over, you'd better kiss me."

"Yes, Ma'am. Ever obedient to your every wish."

He kissed her long and hard.

Kristin hardly noticed them, and Jason had eyes only for her. The room always seemed to light up when he saw her, and a part of him that he didn't even know was tense just eased away.

Without any words, they embraced and their kiss was long and deep.

* * * *

Ferdinand I of Aragon, the Emperor of the De Soto Empire commed his secretary again. "I summoned Enrique Balboa over an hour ago. Where the hell is he?"

The secretary replied, "I have no idea, Your Majesty. I've tried to contact him several times, and no one over at the Security Office knows where he is."

"Well, the moment he reports in, have him come and see me. He has some significant explaining to do."

"Yes, Your Majesty."

The Emperor slumped back in his throne-like chair and simmered. This whole assassination debacle had been Balboa's idea, and Ferdinand intended to demand explanations.

"And that son of a bitch better have some good answers!"

"I don't think he's going to answer you at all, Your Majesty," a strange voice said from the shadows near the window.

The Emperor sat bolt upright and started to reach for his alarm button to call his guards. A shuriken suddenly appeared between his hand and the button.

The same voice said, "I suggest you don't call your guards until you've heard what I have to say, Ferdinand."

A man came out of the shadows. He was medium height, with graying black hair. His clothes were dark, but not particularly unusual. Thousands on the streets could be dressed similarly. But his eyes were the coldest that the Emperor had ever seen, even among his battle commanders and secret police.

The ruler of a vast empire started hotly, "No one calls me by my given name. I am the Emperor!"

The man gave a faint smile.

"Oddly enough, I already knew that, Ferdinand." He gave a grim smile. "And I am Temujin Hawke, the patriarch of the oldest and best family of assassins in the galaxy."

Hawke brought a cloth bag from behind him and dropped it on the Emperor's desk with a dull thud.

"Your man, Juan de Balboa, tried to hire me. When I refused, he tried to kill me and my family." Temujin opened the bag and upended it. A severed head rolled out across the surface of the desk. "He failed."

Ferdinand looked with horror at the gaping eyes of his Director of Security.

Hawke slapped his hand on the desk to get the Emperor's attention. When the ruler looked up at him with startled eyes, the beginning of real fear in them, Temujin said, "At this time, I am assuming that the threat to my family began and ended with the late, unlamented Enrique Balboa. I do not hold you to blame."

He gave the Emperor a look that would have frozen a tropical paradise. "But I promise you, if there is ever another attempt from your Empire on my family, I will kill you and your entire family."

The man turned and faded back into the shadows.

"Only a fool would threaten the Hawke Clan. Are you such a fool, Ferdinand?"

He was gone.

It took over two minutes for the Emperor of the De Soto Empire to finally push the buzzer for his guards. But though they searched the room thoroughly, they found no trace of Temujin Hawke.

He had vanished.

# ABOUT THE AUTHOR

Ed Sutter is a twenty plus year student of the martial arts of Chinese Kenpo, karate, Aikido, and ninjutsu. An alumnus of the Marine Corps, he has worked as a technician, an engineer, a truck driver, a manager, and an estimator. Ed lives in Arizona and actually likes the hot weather.

His interests are reading (big surprise!), writing, history, archaeology, theoretical physics, anthropology, paleontology, golf, skiing, and scuba diving.

*For your reading pleasure, we invite you to visit our web bookstore*